About the Author

G A Reid has worked in Criminal Law practice for over a decade and has used many of her own experiences in her writing. She was brought up in the north of the country, moving to London in her teens. She is married and continues to work part time as a lawyer whilst using her spare time to write. This is the first book that she has published.

Dedication

I would like to dedicate this book to all my family and friends who have supported me through thick and thin. To those who lived my nightmares with me and are still around to tell the tale. A particular acknowledgement must go to my parents and sister for their unconditional love which quite frankly, at times, has kept me sane. Finally to my amazing husband who brought me back to life.

G.A. Reid

ASSOCIATION

AUSTIN MACAULEY
PUBLISHERS LTD.

A CIP catalogue record for this title is available from the British Library.

ISBN 9781784551797

www.austinmacauley.com

First Published (2015)
Austin Macauley Publishers Ltd.
25 Canada Square
Canary Wharf
London
E14 5LB

Printed and bound in Great Britain

CHAPTER 1

BANG! BANG! BANG! Rebecca shot up in bed and grabbed her mobile phone squinting as she looked at the time... 620AM. She heard the noise again. BANG! BANG! BANG! Someone or something was bashing on the front door. Rebecca got up and stumbled to the window, disorientated, still trying to wake up. She pulled the curtain slightly to one side and looked out through the window down to the pavement outside. Seven men and a woman were standing there. One man looked up as Rebecca peered down. They locked eyes, he held up a badge from around his neck and shouted, 'POLICE!' Rebecca let go of the curtain and grabbed her dressing down as she walked downstairs to open the door. She was just on autopilot – her body was moving but she wasn't registering what was happening. She wasn't even able to think ... has something happened to somebody? Is a member of my family hurt? What are they doing here? It was as if her mind was blank.

She opened the front door.

'Rebecca Turner?' the man who held up the badge said.

'Yes,' she replied slowly. He was an old rough looking man with an earring in his left ear. He had balding grey hair and a wrinkled, weathered face with sagging jowls. 'Come in,' Rebecca asked as she opened the door wider.

The seven men and woman trooped into the front room. 'Sit down.' Rebecca gestured towards the sofa as she offered them a seat. It was a natural reaction. The reality of the situation still hadn't hit her. The men looked at each other uncomfortably as if it wasn't appropriate to accept. Rebecca noticed the look then realised something was seriously wrong.

'I'm DC Moran,' said the old officer who had done all the talking so far. He stepped towards Rebecca. 'I'm here to arrest you. I'm arresting you on suspicion of perverting the course of justice in the case of Suri Lee and further arresting you on suspicion of assisting Raj Lee to put money from drug dealing into cars and property. I have to caution you. You do not have to say anything but it may harm your defence if you do not mention when questioned something which you later rely on in court. Anything you do say may be given in evidence.'

'OK,' Rebecca replied slowly, not quite believing what was happening to her.

'You don't look very shocked, were you expecting us?' one officer commented snidely. Rebecca just looked at the officer and said nothing. Nothing was registering. It was as if she could see what was happening but could not feel any emotion about it. She couldn't cry, she couldn't scream, she couldn't even think of anything to ask.

'Where is all your paperwork on Raj Lee?' asked the officer who had made the earlier comment.

'Paperwork? I don't have any. We broke up years ago,' she managed to reply. She was confused. Why would she have any paperwork on Raj Lee? What was going on? What did the police *think* was going on?

The officers began to disperse around the house looking through any draw, box or cupboard they came across. DC Moran told Rebecca to go and get dressed. She would have to come to the station.

She walked upstairs and asked the female officer standing at the top of the stairs, who had been assigned to supervise her, if she was allowed to brush her teeth. It probably seemed like a ridiculous question but Rebecca remembered clients telling her that they were taken straight to the station and not allowed to get changed or washed beforehand. Strangely, brushing her teeth seemed to be the most important thing right now. In the scheme of things this concern was completely irrational but it seemed normal to her right now. Rebecca tried to be practical. She remembered clients moaning about being absolutely freezing in the cells; she put on two jumpers, a coat, scarf and gloves. Rebecca got dressed in a zombie-like state whilst the female officer waited outside her bedroom watching her. When she was ready she walked down stairs with the officer following her uncomfortably closely behind. She was a particularly unattractive woman, very tall with a large bottom. She had pale freckly skin with a hair lip. Her speech was slightly slurred with a lisp.

Rebecca was escorted to an unmarked blue Astra parked outside her home. DC Moran opened the back passenger door and she got in. DC Moran got into the driver's seat and the female officer got into the front passenger seat. No one spoke. Rebecca just stared out of the window. The reality of what was happening still hadn't hit her.

CHAPTER TWO

Rebecca heard the postman at the door. She ran down the stairs and picked up the bundle of letters from the floor behind the door. As she shuffled through the letters she spotted one addressed to her with a London postmark. She just knew it was it. It was exactly what she had been waiting two weeks and 3 days for...every morning. She sprinted upstairs and left the other letters on the dining room table as she passed. She jumped on her bed, letter in hand, took a deep breath and opened it.

Dear Miss Turner, I am pleased to inform you that you have a place at The School of Law beginning September 2001.

Rebecca screamed and read on.

You will be taking a full time place on the Bar Vocational Course.

Rebecca had always wanted to be a barrister. Since she could talk everyone had always said she could argue black was white. Her dream was finally coming true. All the hard work was beginning to pay off. The countless essays, days and days of study and hours of revision and exams. The School of Law was the best law school in the country and was regarded highly by all the reputable barristers, QCs and judges. It had been the only school to run the bar course for many years and was where most of the more established barristers were trained. Rebecca knew that her family, especially her mum and dad, would be so proud of her. They encouraged her to go into law and had supported her emotionally and financially through university. She had worked part time since she was fifteen years old at a local leisure centre with a bowling alley, cinema and restaurants but had still had to depend on her parents to help her pay her way. Things were just so expensive. They had had to pay her university fees as she simply could not afford them on her wage. She knew that her parents had to be the first people she would tell the good news to. She ran down stairs and grabbed the phone. She called her mother at work.

'That's fantastic! Brilliant!' said Anne. 'This is the first step!' Anne had such faith and confidence in Rebecca. She had never doubted for one minute that Rebecca wouldn't make it as a barrister or that she wouldn't be successful. Rebecca finished the call and rang her father, Peter. He was at work too.

'Well done,' he said, 'I *really* am pleased.' Rebecca was pleased too, in fact she was over the moon. She could see her dream was within her grasp now.

Rebecca always had a strong friendship group and was very close to her younger sister, Marie. They were close in age and so had similar interests. Although they were very different in personality and bickered like sisters do, they were best friends. Close as close could be. They shared everything. Rebecca had always been the social organiser of the group. She was a social butterfly. She was a very happy, bubbly person who rarely let anything bother her. She cared about her friends and family very much and would do anything to help any of them. She was always the one that people went to should they need a shoulder to cry on or a lift to the train station. Rebecca liked that she was a reliable friend and that she had so many people that she cared about and who cared for her in return. Her friends were ones that she had had for many years. They had grown up together and knew each other inside out.

Every weekend the group of girls went out into town and partied like all twenty-one-year-olds did. Lots of alcohol, lots of dancing and lots of laughs. They were at an age when they could party Thursday to Sunday and never seem to have a hangover. They all loved the party scene and were regular faces in the bars, pubs and clubs in town. The group of ten girls always included Rebecca, Marie, Jennifer, Nicola, Annette and Anita. They were the members of the group that you could guarantee would be out almost every night enjoying themselves.

'Menzies? Where is it again?' Marie asked Rebecca.

'It's the old church. It's been done up and turned into a club! Opening night is Thursday and guess who has some tiiiicccccckkkkeeetttts?' Rebecca grinned as she fanned open six tickets in front of Marie's face.

'OOOhhhhh count me in!' Marie squealed.

Rebecca lived with her family including Marie in a semi-detached house near the centre of town. Her parents owned a house in the north where they spent most weekends. The girls all started any night out at Rebecca's house. It was a ritual. They had a few drinks, gave each other outfit advice and sorted out each other's hair. Thursday night was no different. One by one the girls arrived dressed to the nines and ready to party. After the usual hair and outfit fiasco they left – later than planned, as usual, and went straight to the club. Leaving the house that night no one had any idea that something so significant was about to happen.

As they stood in the queue the girls chatted away and saw friendly familiar faces from the local area. They got into the club and were having a fantastic night dancing and drinking together.

After a dance it was time for another drink. 'My round,' Rebecca yelled. 'Same?' Everyone nodded and carried on dancing. Rebecca made her way to the bar and saw that it was three people deep. She was undeterred. She was used to this and she had something to celebrate. Rebecca squeezed in between people to the bar. She turned to her left and said, 'Hi,' to the unknown male standing next to her. This was a little distraction technique Rebecca used so that people didn't focus on the fact that she had just pushed past so many people queuing. Be friendly and chat, that was her plan. She had never seen this man before which was quite unusual in the town. He must be here for the opening night she thought to herself. He smiled at her and she smiled back. He was a tall Asian male about 6'2 with dark hair and dark features. Rebecca liked him almost immediately. She felt drawn to him somehow. They chatted while they waited for their drinks. No uncomfortable silences. Of course this could have had something to do with the alcohol she had consumed but Rebecca felt it was more than this. The man told her his name was Raj. After Rebecca had bought the drinks for her friends, she took them over... 'Just chatting to a hottie!!!' She laughed as she returned to Raj who was waiting. They spent the night chatting, laughing and joking. She had a good time with him. There was a definite connection between them. A chemistry that just couldn't be described. As the night came to an end Raj asked for Rebecca's number. Why not? she thought, We got on well - what harm it could do? How wrong could she be?

CHAPTER THREE

Rebecca was running around trying to find the top she wanted to wear. Raj was picking her up in ten minutes for their first date. They had been texting and talking on the phone for over a week and had finally made arrangements to meet up. She had no idea where they were going but she felt a bit nervous. She had butterflies in her stomach. She heard a car pull up outside and heard a beep. She looked through the window and saw a dark blue car with Raj sitting behind the wheel. She shouted goodbye and ran out to the car.

'Hi.' She giggled as she got in the car.

'Where do you want to go?' he asked. They decided to go for a drink in the city. On the journey Raj's phone rang with friends asking him what he was up to. He told them he would be around later on in the evening to play pool. Rebecca thought he must have been expecting a short date as it was already late afternoon. That doesn't sound promising she thought. They went into a bar and chatted over a drink. Raj told her he bought and sold cars for a living. He had his own business and seemed to know what he was talking about. Rebecca told Raj about her plans to become a barrister and her dream to work in criminal defence. They chatted for what seemed like minutes. When Rebecca looked at her watch she saw they had been in the bar for hours.

'Don't you have to meet your friends?' she asked.

'Why? What time is it?' he replied. Raj couldn't believe how quickly the time had gone. They headed back to town. Both of them had had a great time. Rebecca could tell. They felt so comfortable with each other right from the start.

As time went on Raj and Rebecca spent more and more time together. They started seeing each other officially. They still had their weekend nights out separately with their friends and spent the day time apart when Rebecca started Law School. They were just like any normal couple going to the cinema or out for meals. The main difference was that Raj's parents were not told about Rebecca. Raj was a Sikh and his parents wanted him to marry someone from the same religion and caste. It was what was expected of him as the oldest boy in the family. It did not really bother Rebecca at first as the relationship was not necessarily going anywhere. It hadn't got to the stage where she wanted to meet or know anything about his family. It was the honeymoon stage and she was just enjoying being with him. She used to drop Raj off around the corner from his house so that his family did not see her. Once or twice there had been a near miss when she had dropped him off and his sisters had driven up the road. She had had to duck down to avoid being seen. Raj always seemed flustered afterwards. He always told her that his parents wouldn't accept her. They had already tried to set him up with people for an arranged marriage in the past and he had refused to go home and meet his prospective bride. Raj had never been interested in girls, he simply had just not bothered. He had never had a long term relationship and had never wanted one until now. Raj didn't try to hide Rebecca in public but would avoid places where he might be seen by family or family friends who would report back. Rebecca didn't really know anything about Raj's family. She knew he had an older and younger sister and a brother but that was only because she had asked questions. He had never volunteered information to her about them. She saw that he was like this with everyone. He never discussed his family with anyone. Their issues and problems stayed between them only. If Rebecca asked questions he would often say she was cross examining him –

like in her studies. He would tell her things were none of her business. Rebecca knew other Asian families in the local area who were similar in their values and so didn't think anything of it. He was just a very private person. She accepted that. He wasn't a gossip and wouldn't really talk about other people. Raj once told Rebecca that his sister had had a baby, but he had never even mentioned that she was pregnant. This was typical of Raj and Rebecca got used to it. It was just the way he was. She put a lot of it down to his culture and how he had been brought up. Just like the fact that he couldn't tell his family about her, it was just the way it was. The cultural differences didn't seem to be a real problem at the beginning but as time went on they became more obvious. This was mainly in respect to their morals and values.

Raj kept his friends almost completely separate from Rebecca; he also didn't mix with her friends. Rebecca was only twenty-two and this suited her. She was happy to go out with friends at the weekend and leave Raj with his friends. They never mixed in couples. Rebecca's friends didn't really get to know Raj because of this and his friends did not get to know her. There were a couple of friends of Raj that Rebecca realised she knew before they got together. She got on well with them but saw them rarely and only when Raj allowed them to mix. Rebecca was happy with things being separate, it suited her lifestyle. She was a social butterfly who was always out with friends and family. She liked that Raj wasn't needy and dependent on her and had his own life to deal with.

After about six months together problems began in the relationship. The first flush of love and excitement was over and reality was beginning to settle in. Raj had started to become depressed. He would be quite off with Rebecca at times and they started seeing each other less and less. A few times a week they would meet up for a few hours but Rebecca always felt that she irritated him and he did not enjoy the time they spent together. Doing things together had become more of a chore and she sometimes dreaded seeing him. She never knew how he would be with her from one day to the next.

One day Rebecca picked him up and, out of the blue, he told her that he didn't know how he felt about her anymore. He didn't know if he loved her or not. He told her it was over. Rebecca cried and asked if this was for good and if this was a permanent split. She needed to know if this was just him having a bad day taking things out on her. Over the months they had joked with each other and told half truths. The other person would only know that it was a lie if the other person wouldn't say 'I swear'. It sounded silly but it was their little thing that meant something to them both. You never say I swear if you are not telling the truth. 'Swear it's over for good?' Rebecca asked.

'I'm not doing that,' Raj replied.

'Please,' she said, 'then I can deal with it and accept it.' Despite her pleading Raj would not swear it was for good. It was a way of keeping Rebecca hanging, hoping that things could be sorted out and they could be together again. Raj got out of the car and left Rebecca devastated and confused. He had been so cold and had thought nothing of telling her he didn't love her any more. Those words broke Rebecca's heart. She cried herself to sleep that night. Rebecca had always been a confident, happy person but her relationship with Raj was making her insecure. She was changing as a person because she was so unhappy. She was miserable with her family and was snappy and irritable most of the time. They were starting to notice that she wasn't herself. They were getting the brunt of her misery and she was pushing them away, becoming more and more distant with them.

Weeks went by without any word from Raj. Rebecca had lost weight from the split, she was so unhappy. She realised that she would have to get on with her life without him. She loved him so it was so hard to do. She didn't attempt to contact Raj. In her eyes if someone tells you they don't love you and don't want to be with you any more there is no point discussing things and going over and over it in your head. You just have to face up to it and get on with your life no matter how much it hurts.

Rebecca had spent the last few Saturday nights, as usual, at Menzies with Marie, Nicola, Jennifer and Anita. Rebecca had slowly started to enjoy herself again and could relax as she knew that she wouldn't have to face Raj as he always socialised with his friends out of the town these days.

Anne and Peter had relocated to their house up north. They had sold the family home and arranged for Rebecca and Marie to rent a flat together. Rebecca was excited. Living with Marie was going to be fun. They were both single now and could enjoy going out and socialising together. Although she would miss Anne and Peter, she was relieved that she wouldn't have to live with them. Her emotions were so up and down that she found herself snapping at everyone. Everyone aggravated her. She knew it wasn't them. It was her. She was taking her heartbreak out on them but she just couldn't seem to stop herself. It was coming between her and her family. At least if Anne and Peter weren't around, she couldn't take things out on them.

After a month of being single, the girls all headed out into town. They had visited the usual bars and seen the same regular people. They ended up in Menzies. As the night went on Rebecca spotted a familiar figure across the club. It was Raj. Rebecca's stomach turned, she had butterflies. What the hell was he doing here? She told all her friends that she had seen him.

'Right we are going.' 'He's only come here to ruin your night.' They all chipped in.

They made their way to the other side of the club. As they were walking Raj approached Rebecca with a single red rose. 'I'm sorry,' he said as he held the rose towards her. 'I was just depressed, I didn't know what I was saying.'

Rebecca knew she shouldn't make it that easy for him but she couldn't stop herself. She smiled and took the rose. 'That's okay,' she said.

It wasn't OK really. Raj had no idea how devastated she had been. No idea how much she had cried or how little she had eaten. She remembered waking up one morning and forgetting it all for just a second and then it all came flooding back. It felt like it had happened all over again. No one could really understand how she felt unless they had been hurt like that themselves.

Things carried on with Raj and Rebecca for the next few weeks with them getting on well just like at the beginning. Marie wasn't so fond of Raj. She couldn't really forgive him for hurting her sister. She had had to live with Rebecca during those few weeks and had seen with her own eyes how much he had hurt her. Her feelings towards Raj just made Rebecca push her away. She stopped talking to her sister about her relationship as she didn't want her sister to hate him.

After a few weeks things started to deteriorate between the couple again. Raj once again became distant and Rebecca felt more of a nuisance than a girlfriend, asking when she would see him next and hearing his reply... 'Not two days in a row.' She used to feel angry that he could be jokey and happy in front of all his friends and then was quiet and miserable with her. He used to tell her that was how he really felt all the time and that he could be himself with her. Lucky her, she thought. He was depressed again. Sure enough Raj told Rebecca he didn't want to be with her any more. She felt that same pain again. He told her it was for good and said maybe they should see other people. She said she didn't want to. The thought of him doing that made her feel physically sick. Once again Raj wouldn't swear that it was over for good. This meant Rebecca always had a slight bit of hope that they could reconcile.

Contact stopped from that day. Rebecca's friends and family once again had to see her cope with her heartbreak and struggle to carry on with her studies and part time job. Sure enough two months on Raj turned up again, just as Rebecca was starting to feel herself again. He came with his sorrys and his excuses that he was depressed. He said this time he needed to get help and wanted Rebecca to be there with him. Rebecca agreed; she put the way he was acting down to his illness. He said he couldn't feel emotions about anything or anyone.

Rebecca thought that if they got him help, he would be back to the old Raj that she had fallen in love with and the one that she still saw from time to time when he had a good day.

They went together to see his GP, who prescribed anti-depressants. At first they worked fantastically and Raj felt great. Rebecca loved seeing the old him. They spent more time together as they were getting on so well. The tablet's effects soon lessened and Raj's mood became lower and lower. Rebecca knew what was coming. 'I just want to be on my own.'

Rebecca felt that feeling that had become familiar to her. The feeling when your heart physically hurts from the upset and you feel desperate to offer a solution to sort things out. She knew there was no point. When Raj was like this he couldn't be persuaded to think things through.

Weeks on, a note was pushed through Rebecca's door.

Rebecca ring me, I understand if you don't.

Enough is enough Rebecca thought, I'm not ringing him.

CHAPTER FOUR

Rebecca was sitting in her flat forcing herself to eat her dinner. Her appetite was all over the place. When she was happy it was fine but during her breakups with Raj it was a struggle to eat. As she pushed the food around her plate she heard a car beep outside. She didn't turn around at first. The car continued to beep faster and faster. She turned and looked out of the window. Raj was outside in his car. He had seen her turn. He knew that she had seen him. He kept on beeping and beckoned her through his driver's window. She just ignored him and turned back around. What is he doing? she thought. Seconds later Rebecca's phone started to ring. She looked at the screen and saw it was Raj. She answered.

'Please,' he begged, 'I just don't know what's wrong with me. I keep having panic attacks. I can't even drive without feeling claustrophobic. I need your help. I need to go and see someone. Please.'

He sounded so distraught and upset. She couldn't just turn him away. 'I'll come down,' Rebecca said. She had no emotion in her voice. She was just so tired of all the drama.

She went outside and got in the car. She didn't say a word. 'Can we go and walk?' Raj pleaded. They walked up to a park where Raj told Rebecca that he had been having panic attacks. 'I can't carry on like this.' He sobbed. He asked if she could help him find someone to go and see. Rebecca knew she should tell him he wasn't her problem any more but felt that she couldn't leave him when he had come to her at his most vulnerable. 'I'm just not myself,' he explained, 'but I love you and have really missed you.' Rebecca accepted what he was saying just like she always did. He never really had to work hard to get her back. He used his health and vulnerability. She didn't have the heart to cut him off no matter how many times he had done it to her.

Rebecca set about trying to find names of consultants that Raj could be referred to. She had a feeling that Raj needed her and she had to stand by him no matter what he had put her through.

So the pattern continued, month after month, year after year. They spent as much time apart as they did as a couple. Rebecca was dropped and picked up whenever Raj felt like it. He had no regard for how it was affecting her or how traumatic it was every time. Even at their best times, Raj never made Rebecca feel loved. She started to feel insecure and was constantly on egg shells always waiting for the next time he would leave her. Raj never showed her any affection. She put this down to his culture, where it would be unusual for his family to hug or tell each other that they cared. Most men Rebecca had dated did not talk about their emotions but Raj was on a different scale.

From one day to the next Rebecca did not know how he felt about her. His actions suggested that he did not care. He prioritised his friends and did not seem to enjoy the time they spent together. Despite all this Rebecca could not leave him. He had a hold over her that she simply could not break. She justified this to herself by saying that she could trust him 100% and that he would never cheat on her. Rebecca rationalised that that would be the worst thing he could do to her. As Raj paid no attention to other females Rebecca strangely felt that she was lucky to have him. It was perverse but she couldn't see it.

Raj frequently put her down so that her confidence was low... 'Fat little shit, look at your chipped tooth.' He would laugh at her. She never wanted him to see her not looking her best so always had her hair and make-up done whenever she saw him. It wasn't the real her but she couldn't bear him to see her naturally. She wasn't confident enough. He never paid her any compliments... she just felt unattractive all the time. He used to talk about how attractive he was and that just made her feel worse. I'm punching way above my weight here, she thought. He's way out of my league. He had completely managed to manipulate her. He had changed her from a strong, independent, bubbly individual to an insecure, unhappy girl. She barely recognised herself but couldn't seem to get herself out of it. It was indescribable.

One evening Raj had reluctantly agreed to drop Rebecca and her friends off to a club out of town. He had picked them all up from Rebecca's house. They were all so excited about going somewhere new. Rebecca was wearing a brown suede skirt that she had bought to wear with her boots. She was excited about Raj seeing her dressed up. She hoped he might even say she looked nice. As she got into the car she could tell he was not happy. He was quiet all the way to the club and pulled away when she tried to touch his hand. He didn't say anything until Rebecca's friends had got out of the car. 'What are you wearing?' he spat with disgust.

'Er, my new skirt?' she stuttered.

'You're a slag wearing that, you're embarrassing me. Get out, it's over.' He looked away. Rebecca did not know what to do. She felt desperate. She felt a lump in her throat and she fought back tears. She couldn't leave her friends and go home to change when they had travelled together so far out of town. She tried to reason with him but he repeatedly told her to get out. She got out of the car in tears. Her night was ruined and her relationship was over yet again.

Raj wouldn't like Rebecca wearing skirts or dressing up when she went out. He would put her down and threaten to finish with her if she dressed like that. He was slowly controlling every aspect of her life.

Issues continued to occur between the couple. Raj had humiliated Rebecca publicly so many times that it just became the norm for her now. She worried that people would be laughing at her behind her back. She knew that people must think she was stupid to put up with it. It was damaging her relationships with her friends. They told her home truths that even though she knew herself deep down, she wasn't ready to hear from other people. She reacted by distancing herself from everyone. She stopped telling them when Raj had made her cry or let her down.

Rebecca always wanted to spend birthdays together but Raj wanted to be with his friends. They were his priority. Rebecca managed to persuade Raj to let her come out with his friends. The friends that Raj was so eager to spend his birthday with Rebecca had never met before. They had been dating for the past two years and she still found out new things about him every day.

Once they got into Menzies Rebecca took everyone's orders and went to the bar. She was really trying with Raj's friends. She wanted them to like her. 'Maybe he will let me come out more with him if we all have a good time?' she reasoned with herself.

Her phone rang. It was Anita. 'Where are you?' she asked.

'I'm in Menzies with Raj,' Rebecca replied cheerily.

'Raj is in here,' replied Anita confused. Anita was in another local club round the corner. Rebecca felt humiliated and angry. 'Right, I'm coming there.' She could not believe that Raj had just left her in a nightclub on her own. Why had he done that? Everything was going well? She didn't understand.

She stormed into the club and saw Raj straight away near the bar. She marched up to him and screamed, 'I hate you! Why did you just leave me?' He just laughed at her as she was pulled away by her friends. The door staff told her to calm down. She looked like the crazy one. She looked like she was the one in the wrong. She felt completely humiliated again. He had obviously persuaded his friends to leave with him, knowing she had gone to the bar to get them all a drink. He did not care about her feelings at all.

She left the club in tears comforted by Anita. 'Why do you put up with it?' Anita asked.

'I honestly don't know.' She sobbed.

Rebecca was always crying and upset throughout the relationship. Rebecca's friends disliked Raj. He made no effort to change their opinion and spent very little time, if any, with her close friendship group. He didn't care about what Rebecca cared about. He wasn't bothered if her friends liked him or not. They were irrelevant to him despite them being so important to Rebecca. She wanted them to all get on but she knew he would never make the effort to do that. Each conversation Rebecca had with her friends about Raj described the arguments they had had or how he was treating her at that time.

Things started to change nearly three years into the relationship. Raj was arrested for fighting after a night out in town. Rebecca was never there when he got into any trouble. He had just told her his side after the event. She knew he had a temper from time to time but put it down to a combination of stupid male ego and alcohol. On most nights out there were fights in town, they became the norm and so no one saw them as a big deal. Rebecca rarely saw Raj out.

One night Raj told Rebecca that he had been bitten on the hand by a friend of a friend after a row. He said he had retaliated by punching the guy in the face. The police had arrived and arrested him. Raj was charged with assault. Rebecca saw the bite mark on Raj's hand and took him to hospital for a tetanus injection. Raj thought he might be able to sort things out with the guy amicably without having to go to court. Despite Rebecca advising him to leave it, he told Rebecca that he was going to see the guy with the mutual friend to try and patch things up. Raj went and said sorry to the guy. The guy said it was in the police's hands now but accepted Raj's apology and shook his hand.

The next day, the police attended Raj's home address and arrested him for witness intimidation. The guy had reported that although Raj did not threaten him, he felt intimidated that

Raj had come to see him and therefore knew where he lived. Raj heard through mutual friends that the guy felt humiliated by being punched by Raj and that he was going to do all he could to make things as worse as possible for him. He had not felt intimidated at all, he just wanted revenge.

The case went to court and as matters were pending Rebecca and Raj's relationship was under added pressure. No matter how hard Rebecca tried to help Raj he just pushed her away and continued to spend more and more time with his friends.

In court, Raj pleaded not guilty to both charges. He believed that he acted in self defence. He did not agree that he had intimidated the witness. He felt like he was being set up. Rebecca supported him. She accepted his account. He had no reason to lie to her.

Rebecca qualified as a solicitor just before the trial date. She had worked hard to get where she was. She was not happy that her boyfriend was being prosecuted for an assault and witness intimidation but she accepted his version of events and believed that he wasn't guilty. She knew it didn't look good because of her role and profession but could not desert Raj when he was under so much pressure.

On the day of the trial, the guy gave his evidence and the District Judge believed his account. Raj was convicted of ABH and witness intimidation. He was sentenced to six months imprisonment. He had never been to prison before and Rebecca was worried about him. She sat through the evidence and felt that the case had been unfair. Although Raj had assaulted the guy, he had done it in self defence and had had two witnesses to confirm his account. Raj had told her that there was more background to the case so she felt that the intimidation was a prime example of the 'victim' playing the system.

Rebecca stood by Raj through his sentence. He ended up serving just six weeks before he was released. Rebecca's thinking was that she had to stand by him. She could not turn her back on someone in a difficult situation.

After Raj's release he finally seemed to realise that Rebecca was there for him and that she genuinely cared about him. He seemed to be more respectful of Rebecca. She noticed a change in him.

Raj decided that he would move out of his parents' house and into a house that his sister had bought to rent out. There was never any consideration of whether Raj and Rebecca should move in together. Despite being together on and off for nearly three years, they were nowhere near that stage in their relationship. They had a very young relationship... almost like they were in their teens.

Once he moved in Rebecca would come and stay from time to time. She remained in her own flat as although they were getting on better than ever, they were still not ready to make that extra commitment. As soon as Raj moved into the house the arguments between Raj and Rebecca almost came to a complete stop. They spent more time together and Raj told her that he had started to feel better. Despite this they still continued to have very independent lives. Rebecca continued to spend time with her friends separately as did Raj.

CHAPTER FIVE

During the course of their relationship, Rebecca had managed to continue with her studies and after a year of assessments, intense exams and a lot of hard work, she successfully completed her bar exams. It was Rebecca's dream to be a barrister and represent people in court. Her passion was for criminal law and she had a particular taste for defence work. Rebecca attended a ceremony where she was called to the Bar. She was formally then recognised as a trainee barrister. Her parents attended the ceremony with her and were so proud of how much she had achieved. Rebecca was so pleased that she was just a step away from her achieving her lifetime goal. Her academic and work life had gone exactly as she had wished but her personal life with Raj continued to be the mess it always had been.

After her academic studies concluded it was time for Rebecca to apply for pupillages and set about getting as much work experience as possible in her preferred field. There was so much competition for work. Rebecca had no connections and did not seem to know the right people to be able to get her foot in the door. She spent months and months making application after application and letter after letter just to be given an interview. It was such hard work. 'It'll all pay off,' she kept telling herself.

The knock backs continued but she refused to give up. She tried to get as much experience as possible, even working for free, to get herself out there. Finally she was given a break by a local firm who sent her to sit behind barristers in Crown Court cases assisting them and making notes for their reference. She loved being in the courtroom and with every day that passed she grew more certain that this was exactly what she wanted to do. She started to work as a county court advocate, part time, dealing with mortgage repossessions and civil small claims. It was at that point Rebecca was certain that she wanted to defend people rather than claim or prosecute against them. She didn't enjoy trying to repossess people's houses, she always felt sorry for the people at court. She wasn't very good at her job as her heart wasn't in it. She knew she wasn't but she just didn't have it in her. Her employers started to notice her lack of enthusiasm and grew increasingly unhappy with the outcome of her hearings. Rebecca decided to stop working for them before they let her go.

Finally, she was offered a full time job as a trainee solicitor with the firm that she had been sitting behind counsel for. Although it had never been Rebecca's ideal to be a solicitor, pupillages were so hard to come by and Rebecca decided she would be in a better position if she got on her feet in court as a solicitor and then reapplied for a pupillage with more court experience under her belt.

She started at Fishbecks Solicitors. She worked long hours and had to undertake further studies to transfer over to work as a solicitor. She loved going to the police station and attending court to represent people. She enjoyed being the voice for those who were often vulnerable and sometimes not educated enough to effectively give their side of the story. Rebecca was always asked by people who found out what she did, 'How can you defend people who you know are guilty?' The answer was simple. 'You can't and you don't.' Everyone Rebecca represented had a side to tell. Rebecca came to realise that it wasn't always as clear cut as Jo public might think. There was often a lot more to each case than first appeared. The police and prosecutors could often be manipulative and economical with the truth. It was the defence's job to make sure the courts had the full facts.

Being a defence solicitor was much more difficult then prosecuting. From the outset they started on the back foot and played catch up. Rebecca found the magistrates in court had no real understanding or empathy with the defendants and many were very prosecution minded. The clerks could be the same. Some of the biased comments made before the cases were called on were unbelievable. 'Why doesn't your client just plead guilty and save us all from wasting our time?' 'How do you sleep at night?' was a comment made by police officers on a regular basis. Rebecca had formed the opinion through personal experience that nine out of ten officers were bent. She had been told 'off the record' endless times that forensic evidence had been planted on suspects 'because it was definitely him but we just couldn't prove it'. She had seen with her own eyes suspects being bundled into the station by several police officers being far too rough using excessive force on the suspect. What do the officers say if suspects complain? They close ranks, write their statements together and hide any incriminating evidence. They set about to humiliate those in custody and treat them as second class citizens. Rebecca knew there were a handful of decent officers who did things by the book and could sometimes see both sides of the coin. Rebecca wasn't blind or naive, she could see that at times people were bang to rights, caught red handed and as guilty as hell. Behind each suspect there was always a story and a background. Rebecca had only come across a handful of clients that she disliked and a couple of them that she felt were a real danger and needed to be locked up for everyone's safety. Rebecca saw the police as the biggest gang in the country. They could do whatever they wanted and it was dangerous to be on the wrong side of them. They had the power to make or destroy a person and that was what they often did.

Despite constantly fighting an uphill battle for clients, Rebecca loved her job. She loved making a difference and fighting for something that she was truly passionate about.

This did not go unnoticed and before long Rebecca was offered several jobs by the top firms working in her area. All mentioned that they had been impressed by her work in court and would like her to come and work for them. Rebecca considered each offer carefully and decided to accept a job at Harters. She liked the people there and although they were not offering as much of a salary as some of the other firms. She felt it was the right decision for her and that she would enjoy working there. Other firms asked her to reconsider her decision and increased their salary offer. When she gave in her resignation at Fishbecks, they asked her to stay and offered her an increase in her salary to stay. But her mind was made up – she was moving forward.

CHAPTER SIX

During the progression in her career, Rebecca's on-off relationship with Raj continued. She managed to put her dramas out of her mind while she was working at court but would always come crashing back to reality once she was out of work hours. When they were having difficulties she always felt on the edge of breaking down but fought to hold it together.

As her career seemed to be taking off, Rebecca decided that it was time to invest and buy a house. She had stopped living with Marie a couple of years earlier when Marie had moved in with her boyfriend, Sam. Rebecca had rented a flat alone since then and enjoyed living on her own. Her friends would call in all the time. She always had something on and something to do. She thought that buying a house was sensible; she needed to think of the future and get on the property ladder. There was no question of whether or not she should buy a house with Raj. He was living in his sister's house and seemed quite happy. They were not stable enough to buy anywhere together. Rebecca knew that it wouldn't be a move that he would want to make with her anyway. That would be investing in their future together and he wasn't sure about how he felt about her from one day to the next.

Rebecca started viewing properties. She went on her own. Her parents were living up north and she was very independent. She didn't even ask Raj if he wanted to come.

He wouldn't be interested because it wasn't about him. He would only criticize the properties that she saw and put them down. Nothing she did was praised by him. It was like he was jealous of her doing well and becoming a success.

After viewing just a few properties, Rebecca saw a small Victorian end of terrace house which she loved. She decided it was perfect for her and put in an offer to buy it. It was still in the same area so she could still be close to everyone. She thought it might be sensible to move out of her rented flat while the house was going through the sale so that she could save every penny for the move. She asked Raj if she could stay with him for a couple of months while she was waiting for the contracts to exchange. He reluctantly agreed. Rebecca did think this was a step forward. A year back she wouldn't have even dared to ask him and although he wasn't exactly enthusiastic about it she saw this as a slight movement forward.

The day that Rebecca moved her stuff into Raj's sister's house was freezing cold and pouring down with rain. Rebecca spent the morning packing her belongings into her car. Most of the furniture was part of the rented flat so she could leave it there. She had sent some smaller items up north with Anne and Peter on their last trip down. It was hard work loading up her car alone. After what seemed like hundreds of trips later Rebecca was all done. She was exhausted and soaking wet.

As Rebecca pulled up at her temporary home Raj didn't come out to greet her. He sat inside the house watching television while Rebecca struggled in the rain to carry her belongings into the house. Things were heavy, Raj could see her but he didn't offer to help. When she got her things upstairs she saw that he had made no room for any of her clothes. He hadn't cleared any space in his drawers or wardrobe despite knowing that she was bringing her things round today. Rebecca put her cases of clothes on the floor in an empty bedroom. She lived out of a suitcase and took clothes out as and when they needed. She did not feel welcome. She felt she could not put her toiletries in the bathroom or her photos and ornaments on display. Most of her belongings were just stored in the garage. None of it was used in the house. It was clear that Rebecca was only there temporarily and that she would never be able to feel like this was her home. It was a pit stop and that was all. Raj wanted to make that obvious.

Rebecca and Raj did not seem to see each other any more than they previously had despite living together. Rebecca went out most night to see her friends. She did not feel able to invite anyone over as it wasn't her home and she felt embarrassed about how she was living. Raj did not do anything to help her settle in. He wouldn't have liked it if she had asked people over as he was so private, he would not have wanted anyone to see in. Her friends wouldn't have felt comfortable anyway. What little they knew of Raj they did not like. They kept their distance just as he kept his. Rebecca was used to that... it was the way it had always been and she just accepted it. It was normal to her now.

Raj had an English bull terrier that lived in the garden of the property. One morning Rebecca looked out of the window and saw that lots of her personal possessions were all over the garden, ripped to pieces or chewed beyond recognition. Rebecca ran downstairs to see that the dog had somehow got into the garage and had destroyed her CDs, DVDs and photos that had been kept there. He had chewed everything. Rebecca cried when she saw what he had done. She was so upset that all her stuff had been damaged. She knew it was no one's fault but couldn't help feeling a bit annoyed that her stuff had been left in the garage like that in the first place. Rebecca took a chewed DVD upstairs to Raj who was still in bed. She showed it to him. He could see that she had been crying. 'Look what he's done,' she said. Raj just laughed. He wasn't bothered. 'Don't you even care about my things?' she cried.

Well what can I do about it?' he said and turned over. Rebecca knew it... he had no respect for her things and he had no respect for her. No more was said about the damage, what was the point? Rebecca did not forget it. It was just another incident stacking up. Rebecca used to say to Raj that he was destroying their relationship and in the end so much damage would be done that it would be too much to fix. He would just tell her to shut up but she knew what she was talking about. She could feel that she was becoming immune to the abuse, she knew that she didn't cry as much anymore not because things didn't happen as often but because she had almost given up caring. Raj was on thin ice. He was so cocky that he didn't even realise it, but they were nearing the end.

When Rebecca lived with Raj, she paid for food and sometimes would contribute towards the bills. She had no idea about the rent. That was between Raj and his sister, Suri. She never got involved. Raj never discussed money or his family with Rebecca. He saw the three things as very separate. Rebecca had learnt this very early on in their relationship. It was none of her business. It never needed to be any of her business as they were always so independent. They had their own lives, it was almost like school dating. Raj got his money from selling cars that he bought from local auctions or from Auto Trader. Rebecca had been there several times when Raj had been to look for cars or had taken someone on a test drive. She never really asked about it and he never spoke about it. She wasn't really interested in his cars. She could see what was going on around her and could hear the phone call enquiries about cars but had no idea of the money involved or how Raj operated his business. They had no financial link... she had no need to know. He didn't know what she earned and she did not know what he earned.

After living at Raj's for a couple of months Rebecca was still unhappy. She was struggling living out of a suitcase and Raj had not offered any more space. Marie came to the rescue; she could see how miserable Rebecca was and offered her a room at her house with Sam until her house sale had gone through. Rebecca jumped at it.

CHAPTER SEVEN

As she moved her belongings out of Raj's house, he once again offered no help and left her struggling and depending on her friends to lend a hand. Rebecca knew it was coming to the end of their relationship. She had put everything she could into it and although Raj had improved towards her since he had been in prison, he still treated her badly by normal standards. It just seemed better to Rebecca because before it had been so awful. Rebecca tried to convince herself that things were really getting there but she knew deep down that the relationship would never work. He just couldn't love her the way she wanted and the way she needed him to. He would never include her in his life the way she wanted. She had started to accept that they were not compatible and things would never work between them. They were just too different, no matter how much she loved him. Anne had always drummed into Rebecca and Marie from an early age that they should, 'be the adored and not the adorer' in a relationship. Rebecca certainly felt that it was the other way round with Raj.

The relationship ended when she moved into Marie's house. She just stopped making the effort and his pride stopped him from making any. Things just petered out into nothing. She continued with her day to day life and adapted to him not being around any more. She was doing OK without him.

After Christmas and months apart, Raj started to call Rebecca. Things slowly fell back to the way they used to be, but Rebecca didn't care the way she used to about him. It had slowly been chipped away over the years. The relationship had turned into more of a habit.

Rebecca continued to socialise weekly with her friends as did Raj. One normal Saturday night, Rebecca had been out for drinks in town with her friend Jennifer. At the end of the night Raj called Rebecca to see what she was up to.

'I'm just in town,' she told him.

'Whereabouts?' he asked. 'We have just been playing snooker and are getting some food; we can drop you home if you want?'

'Great,' thought Rebecca, 'a free ride home.'

Raj pulled up in a car next to Rebecca and Jennifer. He was sitting in the passenger's seat. Rebecca vaguely recognised the driver. There were two people already in the back of the car. Rebecca did not recognise either of them. 'For God's sake, why's he offered to pick us up when there's no room.' She rolled her eyes. She squeezed into the car and Jennifer sat on her knee. 'Hi,' they both said. As they drove to drop Jennifer off at home, there was chit chat between the boys in the car. Rebecca and Jennifer listened but barely said a word.

A blue light appeared behind the car. Those in the back seat turned around and saw a police car flashing behind it and indicating for the driver to pull over. The driver complied. A police officer appeared at the driver's window and looked into the car.

'Just a routine check,' he informed them. 'I'm going to need to take your details,' he said to the driver as he opened the driver's door. 'Can you come with me?' The driver got out of the car and went with the officer to the police car behind.

A second officer appeared at the passenger window and asked for everyone's details. Jennifer and Rebecca gave their names, addresses and dates of birth for the officer's notes. It was just a bit of an inconvenience as the girls wanted to get home.

The driver returned to the car and they continued on their journey. No one thought anything of the car being stopped. It was a routine check like the officer said. It was late at night, the officers were probably bored and looking for something to do, Rebecca thought to herself. Typical.

They dropped Jennifer off and carried on to Marie's where Rebecca thanked the driver, said her goodbyes and got out.

Just a month later, Rebecca's house had completed. She was so excited. She finally had a house all of her very own. She picked up the keys and went round to the property. She had loved the house when she went to view it and couldn't wait to see it again. It seemed so cosy. A real home. When she eagerly opened the front door she could not quite believe what she saw. The place was falling to bits. Things had been hidden by clever decoration by the previous owners during her viewings. The walls were falling to bits, there was woodworm in the flooring and the carpets were heavily stained and worn. Rebecca had been quite naive when viewing the property and as a first time buyer had been taken advantage of. She didn't have anyone to look at the property with her. Her parents lived up north and Raj was certainly not interested in anything that wouldn't benefit him. None of her friends had houses. She should have asked Marie and Sam but she had done it alone... just like she had done with everything. What should have been a happy and exciting day for Rebecca was gutting. She cried as she thought about her house and how much work she would have to do on it. How could she do it? Who could help her? Rebecca worried about how much money she would have to spend on it. She had used all her money to buy the house. Her parents had given her the deposit like they had for Marie, but she had had to pay for the fees involved. It had been a stretch for her. In a normal relationship, people can depend on their partners to help each other but Rebecca was on her own in this relationship. She always had been.

Rebecca had to stay longer at Marie's while she spent every spare moment at the house, painting, plastering and cleaning. Her friends were there to help her but Raj never came round. As far as he was concerned it was nothing to do with him. It was Rebecca's and it was completely separate from him.

Raj never offered help, but as the work was slowly completed Rebecca asked him to do her one favour. 'Please could you put my wardrobe together while I am at work?'

'Yeah sure,' he said. Rebecca was surprised he hadn't refused to or at least moaned about it. She couldn't believe he had agreed so readily. She gave him the key. She could finally see the end of all the work at the house. It was nearly ready for her.

The following night, Raj picked her up from Marie's. As she got in the car, exhausted from her day, Raj held up a screwdriver. 'Let's go and put your wardrobe together.' He smiled.

'Are you joking?' Rebecca was seething.

'No. Why?' answered Raj, not quite seeing what was wrong.

'I asked you to do that today. I haven't asked for your help at all with the house but thought you could do this one thing for me!' Rebecca's voice was shaking with anger.

'Yeah we can do it now,' he said confused.

'I don't want to do it now!!!!' she yelled. 'I wanted you to do this one thing for me! That is it!!' she screamed. 'You are the most useless piece of shit I have ever met!' Rebecca got out of the car and slammed the door behind her. THAT IS IT! she thought to herself. Enough is enough. It was the final straw. In comparison to how Raj had treated her in the past it was a very minor incident, but it finally put everything into perspective for her. Raj was never going to put her first or care about her the way she cared about him. It simply didn't matter to him that something could be important to her.

Rebecca realised this was not what she wanted, it was not the life she wanted; she wanted more.

Raj contacted Rebecca three weeks later, like clockwork. He obviously thought it was just another row and that things would go back to normal. Rebecca stood strong. 'We aren't getting back together,' she told him. 'It's over this time. I've had enough.' Rebecca had never finished the relationship before. This time it was for good. It was over and there was no going back for her.

Much to Rebecca's surprise, Raj started to realise what he had lost and tried to show Rebecca that he loved her and was sorry. He tried to do all the things she had wanted him to do when they were together. Little things like calling her to ask if she needed anything for the house or coming round after a night out. He would throw stones up at her window after a night out and ask to come in. She would send him home as he begged her to talk to him. When they were together she would have to beg him to come over after a night out and then most of the time he wouldn't even bother. Now she couldn't get rid of him. He was making such an effort but it was too little too late; the damage had been done. Raj was devastated. Rebecca was shocked at how much emotion he showed when he realised she had had enough... he did love her after all but he loved himself more. That would never change.

Slowly the realisation hit him that it was over between them.

Raj would still contact Rebecca now and again and she would always answer the phone to him and be there if he needed her. She felt like she couldn't let him down and felt guilty for finishing it and leaving him. These were strange emotions especially considering how he had treated her over the years and how he had just disregarded her feelings so many times with not an ounce of guilt over it. He had hurt her incredibly time and time again but she could not bring herself to do the same to him. She would rather hurt herself than see him suffer. She just could never explain why she felt like this.

CHAPTER EIGHT

Rebecca started work at her new firm, Harters. Rebecca was good at her job and she enjoyed it. She loved working with the clients and seeing a different side of the story to that the police had put their slant on. She actually liked some of the local officers and worked with them well. They had a mutual respect for each other. She knew they wouldn't try and mislead her and they knew that she wasn't one of these bent solicitors that they couldn't trust. She represented her clients, in their best interests but she would do everything by the book – that was her and the police knew it.

The more she worked with the police the more passionate she became about her job. The police were in a position to abuse their power and abuse it they did – constantly. Rebecca could think of two sergeants who were unbiased and could consider each case fairly – every other officer would be desperate to charge every person they arrested regardless of their guilt. It wasn't just statistics for the force, it was like they were programmed from the start to think this way. They treated those who were arrested like rubbish, handled them roughly and colluded with each other maliciously to throw the book at everyone they possibly could. Rebecca wanted to protect her clients and often felt emotionally involved with many of her cases.

She fought so hard to get her client's story heard by magistrates. When she was starting out she believed that she could make a difference but she soon saw how prosecution minded the magistrates and judges could be. Magistrates ALWAYS accept an officer's word. It did not matter how many other people said this was not the case or how unlikely the officer's account was – it was accepted as the gospel truth just because they were in a uniform.

Rebecca was at the police station, one Sunday morning, when she saw young girl in custody wearing a little dress and high-heel shoes. She was distressed and crying. She had make up running down her face. No one acknowledged the distressed girl; it was like she was invisible.

Rebecca went over and sat next to the girl on the bench. 'Don't cry,' she said. The girl looked up and Rebecca smiled. 'You will be OK, trust me.'

The custody sergeant looked over. 'That's one for you,' he said pointing at the girl. Rebecca was duty solicitor and the girl had requested legal representation.

'I'm going to help you, so take a deep breath, calm down and don't worry.' Rebecca went to speak to the officer dealing with the case to get disclosure of some of the facts.

'She bottled two people in a club; both have injuries and have identified her. It's on CCTV too. We haven't got that at the moment but it's clear as day on it. We are going to take the statements from the injured parties later today. She just needs to admit it,' the officer told Rebecca.

'Right, how soon can we get her out of here? Are there going to be any bail issues or can we bail straight after interview for further enquiries?' Rebecca asked.

'Well it should be quite a short interview,' the officer replied. 'I'll bail her straight out. She'll be out of here in a couple of hours at the most.'

Rebecca went into the consultation room with the girl. Her name was Jenny. She explained the allegation to Jenny and asked her what had happened. Jenny was distraught. She was a young, married mum who had been on a rare night out with friends. She had never been in trouble before. 'I didn't bottle anyone, I was trying to stop a fight,' she cried. 'He said people saw me do it so maybe I did? Why would he tell me I did if I didn't? He's a police officer so he must be telling me the truth. I'm just going to go in there and tell him I did it. He told me I had to go in and tell the truth.' Jenny spoke erratically. She was confused about what had happened and what was happening to her.

Officers briefing and frightening suspects was a regular occurrence even though it was against the procedural codes and regulations. Rebecca was not surprised, it was expected. The poor girl was so naive, why would a police officer say something that wasn't true? Because that is what they do Rebecca felt like saying.

'I have just been told you are going to be out of here within a couple of hours,' she told Jenny. 'Now, forget what the officer has said to you, what do you remember? Do you remember hitting anyone with a bottle?'

'No,' said Jenny, 'I'm sure I didn't but I'm just confused as to why people would say these things.'

'Look, if you are sure you didn't hit anyone with the bottle then you are not going in there admitting anything. You are going to be OK.' Jenny felt better that someone believed in her.

They went into interview and Jenny made no comment. She was so unclear as to what had happened and so confused that talking in interview was dangerous. She wasn't guilty but she needed time to think things through and get everything straight in her head.

In interview the officer's face dropped when Rebecca intervened and told him that Jenny would be exercising her right to silence. He was furious.

'Right, you going to bail her now?' Rebecca asked after the interview.

'No,' replied the officer, 'she will have to wait.' The officer was so annoyed that Jenny hadn't done as he had told her in interview that he was going to make her pay by leaving her in a cell for as long as he possibly could. Rebecca shook her head in disgust but there was nothing she could do. The power was all theirs.

The CPS were no different. The police would know who the aggressive charging lawyers were and would wait until they were on shift to take their cases to them so they were guaranteed a charge of the highest possible offence. Some prosecution lawyers wanted a conviction at all costs and, like the police, believed everyone was guilty. These were the people behind the justice system, it was frightening. The worst thing was that Jo public had no idea that this was going on and believed that justice was carried out. Rebecca would encourage people to go and watch for just one day at the back of the magistrates or Crown Court and see how many times the defendant is treated fairly or at least the same as the prosecution, it would soon open their eyes.

Rebecca enjoyed it at Harters, there were girls her age who worked there, everyone got on and there was no back stabbing and bitching like at her old firm. Rebecca couldn't quite believe that it was too good to be true but it was like a little family. She liked her boss a lot too. He could be blunt and hard at times but he was there when you needed him and was the best lawyer she had ever met. Ask him anything and he knew the answer. She was proud to be part of the Harters team.

Rebecca still heard from Raj from time to time. He had got into trouble when the police had stopped him in a car he had just bought. They had thought it was stolen and seized it. They checked it over and found it was legit. Raj was always all over the country buying cars, looking in Auto Trader or local auctions, that was his income. He bought cars, did them up and sold them on. He was good at selling things, he had the gift of the gab and he knew people who could fix anything too difficult on the cars. Raj had a trader's policy to be able to take people on test drives and pick up his new purchases. Rebecca had been to the auctions a few times with Raj and had heard him on the phone to potential buyers. She had heard him putting ads in vehicle magazines. She had never asked any more than what she saw – he sold cars; that was his income it was as simple as that. There was no need to question.

Rebecca was enjoying her life and had got used to Raj not being around. He had mentioned to her that his sister had been arrested. He didn't give any details and Rebecca knew not to ask. Raj only told her what he wanted her to know. He didn't like questions. Rebecca had learnt this when they were together and he used to call her nosey and say she was interrogating him after she had asked anything however simple it may be. He knew where she was if he wanted any advice. She didn't feel concerned. She did not know his sister and had no relationship with her. She knew if it was anything major surely he would tell her about it. He hadn't gone into any detail so she didn't worry.

CHAPTER NINE

Like in any business Raj had to complete his tax returns. He had an accountant that he had been to whilst he had been dating Rebecca. Raj had always dealt with his business himself. Rebecca had left him to it. It didn't affect her. Rebecca had never discussed her work with Raj either. They had their own money, income and work life. That was the way it had always been between them and both of them felt they had no need for it to be any different. Raj was always very careful with his money and wouldn't flash it around or splash cash on expensive indulgent items. He always made sure that Rebecca always paid her way and most of the time she ended up covering more than her fair share. Financially they were both sound and neither of them had any need or desire to depend on the other. Rebecca used to laugh to herself about how tight Raj was. She was never treated or spoilt by him. If he bought a drink he made sure she'd buy him one back. Despite that fact that they had been on and off for four years, because of the amount of splits that they had had, they had never really got much further than the dating stage.

One weekend in May 2007, over a year after they had broken up, Raj rang Rebecca asking her if she could explain what his tax returns were asking for; he told her he didn't understand the complex forms or complicated documents. Rebecca didn't question it. Raj wasn't illiterate but he wasn't academic either and needed help when filling in anything important.

'When I get them sent through I've got to go up to my accountants. It's up north so I don't want to get there and have brought all the wrong things with me. It'd be a wasted journey. I just want you check through them with me.' Rebecca sighed.

Quite frankly it was a chore and she was busy with things in her own life. It was the last thing she wanted to do. She very reluctantly agreed. 'Just bring them round when you get them through from the Inland Revenue and I'll have a look. I don't understand them myself though,' she explained. 'I always got my accountant to do them for me when I was self employed.' Rebecca just felt guilty if she didn't help Raj. He gave off this aura of confidence and ego but inside he was insecure and messed up. She felt sorry for him.

After Rebecca had completed her bar exams she had worked for several local solicitors assisting counsel. She had always been paid directly for her work with a cheque or BACS transfer. She had had to declare her earnings for tax purposes as it wasn't deducted by the solicitors beforehand. Rebecca had given all her invoices and bank statements to Anne and Peter's accountant. He had completed the returns and submitted them for Rebecca. Apart from forwarding the relevant documents and paying the bill, Rebecca hadn't had any involvement.

When Rebecca started working at Fishwicks she had received a further tax return. Rebecca didn't have anything to declare as she was now employed through the PAYE system. She called the tax office and asked what she should do. 'Just write zeros in the boxes and write in the details box nothing to declare,' the lady on the phone had told her, 'return that and we will process it.' That was the only real experience Rebecca had ever had with tax returns but she hoped she would be able to translate and put in simple English to Raj what the form was asking for even if she could not actually answer the questions. 'That is what his accountant is for,' she told herself.

A few days later Rebecca received a text. 'Tax returns are here can you help?' Rebecca had been having a bad day. It was really busy at work and she was tired. The last thing she wanted to do with her evening was to translate tax returns for her ex for a business she had nothing to do with. 'Oh can't someone else help you with it?' Rebecca typed.

'You're so miserable,' Raj responded, 'don't worry I'll get my mate to do it.'

Rebecca felt guilty for not helping Raj. He had only asked her to help him to understand a form. She knew Raj wouldn't really feel comfortable asking a friend for help. He was proud and didn't like admitting that he couldn't do something for himself. He would also be embarrassed that he couldn't understand the form himself.

'Alright, just come round later after work,' Rebecca sent back.

Later that night, Raj knocked on Rebecca's door. 'Come in,' she shouted from the couch. Raj had a carrier bag full of forms, documents and receipts. They weren't in any order. Rebecca pulled a couple out and sighed. It was all in a big mess.

'You will have to take these to your accountant,' she told him. She didn't have the time, patience or knowledge to make sense of the documents. That was not what she was there for anyway. Raj sat down on the sofa facing Rebecca. He placed a number of tax returns and a letter from the Inland Revenue on the coffee table in between the two sofas where they both sat. Rebecca picked the forms up. She read through the letter. The most recent tax return was due – it was late in fact and Raj had to pay a £100 penalty charge. The return was for the year 2005/2006, it should have been submitted by January 2007.

The letter was threatening Raj with a home visit if he did not complete and return the forms.

'This is the form they are most concerned about,' Rebecca told Raj. She picked up a form for the years 2000/2001 and frowned. 'This was so long ago, why hasn't this been submitted before?' she asked. Rebecca didn't even know Raj then. She had met him in 2001. He had always sold cars since she had known him and had only in the last year been employed at a local car auction.

He had told her in the past that he had had other jobs. 'I didn't make anything in that year,' Raj shrugged. 'I wasn't actually selling cars then.'

'OK, so you didn't have any income?' Rebecca asked

'No,' Raj responded.

'OK well I know what to do with that form then.' Rebecca remembered what the lady at the tax office had told her years before. 'If you didn't have any income for that year just write in zeros and in the detail box write nothing to declare.' She wrote the zeros in as she recalled and handed the form to Raj. 'I think that's right,' she assured him. 'That's what I had to do.'

Rebecca then picked up the 2005/2006 return that the Inland Revenue seemed most concerned with.

'I don't know what it's asking me for,' Raj said. 'I don't know what I need to take with me.'

'Well take this bag with you,' Rebecca said as she held up the carrier bag of papers. 'Look,' she told him. She read through each question with Raj and simplified it for him. 'I don't know how to fill this form in,' she told him. 'Ill summarise your info on the back of the letter from the Inland Revenue and you will have to leave it to your accountant. OK, what did you earn in 2005?'

Raj reeled off some figures that Rebecca jotted down on the piece of paper. She wrote it under the heading 'INCOME'.

'What did you pay out for this year?' Rebecca referred to the tax return that had direction specifically for the motor trade. 'What did you pay out for MOTs? How much did you pay on advertising? How much did it cost you to travel to pick up cars that year?' Rebecca jotted down Raj's answers. They were rough calculations based on Raj's information. 'Well I did 12 MOTS that year,' he told her, 'and they were about £35 each.' He did the calculation on his mobile phone and read out the answer. Rebecca jotted it down. 'Your accountant will have to see what is deductible according to your receipts.'

Rebecca deducted the total expenses from the total income. It looked like Raj had made £40,000 profit that year. That seemed reasonable to Rebecca. She knew Raj had lots of cars all lined up opposite the fire station in town. He also had cars parked outside his parents' house and at his sisters, where he had lived. Rebecca had earned about £42,000 that year. That seemed like a normal income to her.

'Right,' she told Raj, handing him the scrap of paper that she had jotted his calculations down on. 'I don't think I can do anything else. Just take your rough calculations and receipts to the accountant and see what he says.'

Raj thanked Rebecca and left. Rebecca was glad she had helped her friend. She would have helped anyone who had asked her to in the same way. She completed forms every day at work and had to take down people's income and expenses for legal aid applications. They then had to sign them to say that they were true. That was the nature of the job, filling in lots of forms with other people's information. It was second nature to Rebecca. She closed the door behind Raj and didn't give his visit a second thought.

CHAPTER TEN

Rebecca sat in the cell at the police station not quite believing where she was. She kept praying that none of her colleagues or other solicitors from local firms would see her and ask what was going on. Rebecca put her hands in her pocket and felt an old piece of paper. She opened it and saw it was prayers and readings that she had been given the last time she was in church. She held on to it tight, closed her eyes and prayed over and over again. She prayed that someone would realise that there had been a mistake and they would release her and apologise profusely for their terrible error.

Rebecca had been asked if she wanted a solicitor when she was booked into custody. She knew the first rule at the police station was to have a solicitor. She knew first hand that officers could be very manipulative and people often found words were put into their mouths. She knew that everything that she said in interview she would be held to word for word. She wanted a solicitor. Her own stern words to clients echoed in her head. 'Always ask for a solicitor! It will not delay things and keep you in custody any longer. That is a tactic the police use to encourage people to go into interview without legal help. NEVER go in without a solicitor.'

Rebecca wanted her boss, Duncan Harter to represent her, but that would mean him knowing about what was going on. Maybe they just want to talk to me, she tried to fool herself, maybe they will just release me today and that will be the end of it. No one would have to know. What if I did ask for my boss and he is obliged to suspend me at work? I don't know what the office policy is? How would I pay my mortgage? How would I survive financially if I were to be suspended? I haven't done anything wrong she reasoned. I'm not even sure what the allegation is.

Rebecca pushed all her own experience to one side. She knew it didn't matter if she had done something or not – the police can make a case out of nothing. If they want you the power is on their side. Frightening but it's the reality. Rebecca argued with herself about what to do. A million questions went round in her head. It was all just too much. She began to cry.

She heard banging from the cell next door as her 'neighbour' shouted out for attention. He was ignored. She was able to block the sound and only hear a distant thud as her own thoughts became deafening. The metal window in her cell was slid open and the female sergeant who had booked her in peered through.

'Very serious this,' she commented not so helpfully.

'I know.' Rebecca nodded.

'You OK?' she asked, softening.

'I, I, I just don't know what to do.' Her concerns just came flooding out. 'I want a solicitor but I don't want my boss to know at the moment.' The sergeant didn't reply. She just pushed the slot back across and walked away. Rebecca knew really that her boss would find out that she had been arrested even if nothing came of it. Police leaked information all the time when it suited them. He would probably know about it before she had even been released but she couldn't even contemplate this. She had to tell herself this would be OK so that she didn't become hysterical.

It felt like she had been in the cell for hours, days even, when the door finally opened and DC Carter, the female officer from her house, told her to, 'Come on.' Rebecca was wary of walking through the station, scared of who she might see. She was taken to a room where she was processed. Her

DNA, fingerprints and photograph were taken. She felt so humiliated. She had always thought this was so wrong. Why did they have the right to document your details when it hadn't been proven that you had done anything wrong? These were then kept forever on a database. This was an invasion of people's privacy but was accepted as fair and right, it was just another example of the control by the government and police that people do not recognise until they themselves are drawn in. Rebecca remembered people being arrested by mistake, those who had been wrongly identified. Even when, minutes later the mistake was discovered and it was acknowledged that they were completely innocent, their DNA and other details were taken. Once someone was in custody be it right or wrong it was what they were allowed to do. She didn't object about the process. There was nothing she could do. It was out of her control. She would be on that system forever now.

After processing, DC Carter led her through to an interview room. The officer chatted to Rebecca while they waited for DC Moran to arrive. She knew that they had kept her waiting to let her suffer in her own thoughts. They had planned the arrest for some time and so knew exactly what they needed to interview her about. Nothing had changed since then, they just wanted to take their time to make her sweat. DC Carter seemed really friendly and appeared to be on Rebecca's side. She almost seemed sympathetic and understanding. Rebecca needed a friend and for one moment forgot that she was the enemy and wasn't there to help her.

DC Moran shuffled into the interview room holding various bits of paper and four blank interview tapes. He sat at the table facing Rebecca and DC Carter moved next to him. Rebecca wondered what on earth was coming. She still didn't know what she was supposed to have done. She braced herself as DC Moran began recording and introduced himself on tape.

Rebecca was asked about her relationship with Raj. Rebecca had already decided that she would comment fully in interview. She had to tell them the complete truth. She hadn't done anything wrong. It was the only way that they might realise their mistake. She told them that their relationship had finished years ago and that they had a very on and off relationship. She told them all she knew. She had nothing to hide. She was shown various bits of paper that had been seized from Raj's house, some of them were bills or scrap bits of paper with things written on them. Rebecca answered the best she could giving as much information as possible. She wanted to be helpful and tell them all she knew.

She was shown the piece of paper that she had scrawled Raj figures on for him to take to his accountant. She explained what it was and exactly how it was made. She went through what each figure stood for. She still did not see what the problem was. What was she supposed to have done that had ended her up in here? As each forty-five minute tape was changed Rebecca still did not know where this was going and what she was doing there. As the minutes ticked on nothing became any clearer. She was waiting for some bombshell.

Then it came... DC Moran told Rebecca that Raj was a prolific drug dealer. He was adamant that she must have known that. She must have known that because of how major he was. WHAT? she thought. If she wasn't at a police station being interviewed she would have thought that was some sort of joke. Raj was no angel, he could be mean and too handy with his fists after a drunken night out but he was no drug dealer. He didn't touch drugs, he hated them.

His younger brother, Gilly, had been hooked in by heroin and was a hopeless addict. Typically, she hadn't been told any details by Raj but she knew he had a poor relationship with his brother as a result. Rebecca had learned from other people of the trouble his brother caused. She had never discussed this with Raj, he was so defensive of his family and he didn't see it as any of her business. She didn't want to cause an argument and give him an excuse to finish with her again so she avoided the topic. There was no way Raj sold drugs. Raj was with her, she would have seen if something was going on. What had led them to believe this? Had they found drugs on him? Had he been caught on surveillance supplying someone?

DC Moran told her... they had found a lot of money in his sister's bank account and some scales in his sister's house with small traces of drugs on them. 'Is that it?' Rebecca wanted to laugh but this wasn't funny at all. They were serious. They had added two and two and got five. The problem was they believed they were right and nothing was going to divert them from that.

Throughout the interview sarcastic comments were made by DC Moran. As Rebecca told the officers exactly how her relationship had been with Raj it was clear that the officers did not believe a word she was saying. They had conjured up a picture that they had been as thick as thieves spending every waking moment together. The more Rebecca tried to tell them that wasn't true, the more they accused her of trying to distance herself from him. 'Not every day a solicitor gets arrested,' DC Moran sneered. 'You're in deep brown stuff now, ain't ya?' He was enjoying every minute if this and she could see it.

After hours of interrogation, Rebecca still did not know what she was being accused of. She knew they thought Raj had been a major drug dealer and that she had known that but the crime she was supposed to have committed was not clear to her.

After being put back into a cell for hours while the officers deliberated she was bailed. The officers needed to investigate matters further and Rebecca was given a date in several months when she should return to the police station. 'Oh God, it's not going to end today.' The realisation hit her.

'I will tell my boss, he will find out anyway,' she told the officers as she was let out of the building.

'Well he won't hear anything from us.' DC Moran smirked.

'Can I just ask? What exactly am I supposed to have done?' questioned Rebecca.

'Association,' answered DC Moran as he held the door open. Rebecca walked out emotionally and physically exhausted.

It was dark as she walked the three miles home. They had seized her mobile phone to test for evidence. She didn't try to use a payphone to ask someone to pick her up, she didn't want to get a taxi. She needed the walk home alone to register what had just happened to her and how her life was about to change forever.

CHAPTER ELEVEN

Going into work the next day Rebecca was a nervous wreck but she had to hide her feelings. No one at work could know what was going on. She had to plaster on a smile and act as normal as possible. Inside she was hysterical but outside she was happy go lucky and calm. She had told her sister, Marie, what was happening when she had got home that night. She needed to talk to someone about it or she felt like she would go mad. She had to rant at someone and explain how distressed and worried she was feeling. It was like a nightmare, it still hadn't sunk in. She just needed her sister to tell her everything was going to be alright. Marie had called in sick for Rebecca whilst she had been at the police station. Rebecca just couldn't tell her parents, not yet anyway. They would be worried sick and that was the last thing she wanted. It would be better that she knew exactly where this was going to go and exactly what was happening before telling anyone. She didn't want to worry anyone unnecessarily. Rebecca did not even know what she could tell people anyway, she did not understand what was happening herself. Her parents had never had any dealings with the police and like most members of the public believed they were trustworthy and honest. Rebecca understood that this was the view of most of public. But Rebecca knew all those scandals involving the police that were exposed in the press from time to time where just the tip of the iceberg. Unfortunately most of the time the people that are the subjects of police corruption are 'criminals' who are not seen to have a valid voice to speak out against them.

Rebecca worked through the day waiting for the right moment to tell Duncan what had happened. That moment never came. She sat staring at her case files. She couldn't take anything in. She was unable to do any work. Her thoughts were consumed with the investigation against her.

As each day passed she knew she had to tell him and quickly. Her time was running out. She did not believe DC Moran and knew that her arrest would have been leaked. She plucked up the courage to tell Duncan and asked him cheerily if she could have a quick word. She had no idea where to start and broke down in tears before even saying a word. Duncan already knew. He had already been told and was just about to call Rebecca in to find out what was going on. Duncan was fantastic. He promised to support her all the way. He told her he believed in her and she knew he was genuine. She couldn't have asked for a better reaction from him. He knew the sort of person she was. She wasn't this manipulative, evil harlot the police believed she was. She had her ditsy days when she was almost comical with the idiotic things she came out with, but she was good at her job and could be trusted with anything. Rebecca asked Duncan if he would be willing to represent her. He was the only person she would trust with her case. Effectively she was trusting him with her life, she felt safe doing that. She knew if she could be saved, he would be the only one who could do it. She had respect for Duncan: not only was he was an experienced lawyer but he was the best and that's what she needed. She felt relieved that Duncan knew. It was like a huge weight had been lifted.

The girls from the office had seen Rebecca in Duncan's room and could see her distress through the window. They all scurried over as she opened the door. 'What's wrong? What on earth's happened?' They all looked so genuinely concerned. 'I think we need to go for a drink,' Rebecca replied managing a smile.

While waiting for her next date at the police station, Raj called Rebecca on her landline. News of her arrest had spread like wildfire.

'What's going on?' he asked. Rebecca broke down just at the sound of his voice. She had been too scared to call or see him after being arrested. She didn't want the police to try and make anything out of them having contact so she avoided him completely. It was hard. The first thing she had wanted to do was call him and ask him what the hell was going on.

'I'm going to lose everything,' she sobbed, 'that's what's going on. I'm going to lose my house, my job... everything.'

'Why? ...you haven't done anything,' he tried to assure her.

'I know that,' she replied impatiently, 'but that's not how it works. They think I have and they will do everything they can to build a case against me. Don't you see they have already ruined my reputation and career just by arresting me. I'm a defence lawyer, their enemy. They don't care about the truth. Don't contact me again.'

She hung up, distressed. It didn't even occur to her to ask if he had been involved in drugs. She knew it wasn't true... she would have known. She felt frightened that she had even answered the phone to him. This was all his fault, she thought. If I hadn't gone out with him this would not be happening. She knew that if the police thought they had been in contact they would try and use it against her by implying they were plotting defences to the case. She could not risk talking to or seeing him it was too dangerous. Part of her felt that she needed Raj right then, he was the one person that could understand exactly what she was going through, but she couldn't risk it.

Christmas came and passed. Rebecca still hadn't told her parents what was going on. Duncan had told her that it was important that she had that support and so encouraged her to tell them. Rebecca waited until after Christmas and plucked up the courage to ring her mum. As soon as Anne answered the phone Rebecca broke down. Over the next few hours she told her mum about what had been going on. Her mum was worried and upset. This was her daughter, the lawyer. She held it together for Rebecca's sake and told her that everything was going to be fine. They were going to fight this as a family, they were not going to be destroyed by a malicious investigation and witch hunt by the police. She said everything Rebecca needed to hear. Rebecca felt positive for the first time since her arrest. Even though she was an adult the whole thing had made her feel so vulnerable and she needed her parents support and help more than ever.

Between Christmas and New Year, Rebecca didn't go out much. The last thing she felt like doing was celebrating the festive period. She had become wary of drinking alcohol as she felt out of control and on the edge when she did. She could keep herself calm when she was sober. The evening before New Year's Eve, Rebecca was sitting in her lounge watching TV, when she heard a loud knock at the door. She wasn't expecting anyone to come round. She went to the door and saw Raj standing outside.

'What do you want?' She panicked as she looked around to see if anyone was watching. She daren't invite him in. What if someone saw and told the police? What if the police were watching themselves? She was so paranoid of things looking suspicious that she had become irrational.

'What's going on? Raj asked. 'What have you told the police?'

Rebecca was confused by the question. What did he think she had told the police? 'The truth, of course.' She frowned. It was like Raj thought that she had got him into trouble with the police by saying something. 'I can't talk to you,' she told him remembering Duncan's advice to stay away from him. She felt sorry for Raj as he was clearly as confused and worried as she was. She had to protect herself from him but she felt guilty as she closed the door on him. She wanted to talk to him so much, to ask him what was going on, to find out how he felt, but she was too frightened. Rebecca heard Raj shouting angrily at the door as she walked over to the sofa. She heard him calling her names like he used to when they had had an argument.

'Stupid slag!' he yelled. Rebecca heard a kick at the door. Raj had booted the front door in anger. Rebecca was upset. It was the last thing she needed right now. She wanted to help him but she couldn't. She had to put herself first now. Doing just that had got her in this position in the first place.

CHAPTER TWELVE

On the day she was due to return to the police station in late January, Duncan came with Rebecca to represent her. Rebecca had hoped that she would be called before she was due to return and be told that the nightmare was over and that the investigation had been closed. Deep down she knew that was too good to be true. Sure enough the day came when they arrived at the station and were met by DC Moran and his female sidekick DC Carter. As Duncan introduced himself Rebecca felt protected as someone was finally on her side.

They were given copies of Rebecca's bank accounts for the last seven years and were told they had to account for every deposit made during that period. Duncan finally managed to ascertain from the officers that their case was that every penny that she had paid into her bank accounts was from Raj and that she had been laundering this money for him. This is absurd, Rebecca thought. I hadn't even met him when the first deposits were made.

The money was from wages, expenses, money from Anne and Peter, money from family members and money from her friendship group when she had paid upfront for events, outings or holidays. She had been paid back in cash which she then put into her account. How on earth could she prove all that or remember relevant dates of what each payment related to? This would be the case against her and because she had been in a relationship with Raj if she couldn't prove her innocence she was in serious trouble. She hadn't had any time with her accounts to study them or look through diaries to try and cross reference dates. She had just minutes to prepare a defence which would then be her account for the whole case against her. If she then deviated from that in the future she would be accused of lying.

During interview, Duncan advised Rebecca to answer no comment. 'There is no case against you at all. They are just fishing and have delved into all your finances to try and find something that isn't there,' he assured her. Rebecca felt so much better having support at the station. She knew the whole thing was ludicrous but now she had someone she trusted saying the same thing. Finally she didn't feel like she was going crazy any more

In interview, Rebecca answered no comment and Duncan put forward a written statement denying that any money had been given to Rebecca by Raj. It stated that their finances had always been completely separate. It set out the different sources of Rebecca's money and details of who could confirm this.

In reality, Raj was so careful with his money, Rebecca would often describe him as stingy. It was Rebecca who used to treat him to dinners and gifts not the other way round. The police had got the whole thing completely wrong but they thought they were on to a solid case and could not see the truth right in front of them.

Despite being a police officer for almost 30 years, DC Moran stated on tape in interview that it was for Rebecca to prove where all the money that had been paid into her account had come from. He believed that the burden of proof was on the defence. The fundamental basis of the criminal justice system is innocent until proven guilty... the officer did not even know the basic legal principals. What hope have I got with this imbecile investigating the case? thought Rebecca as Duncan had a heated argument with the officer in interview. The officer would not back down... he believed he was right and nothing would change that. Duncan was exasperated with the officer's inability to see that he was completely wrong.

After hours of interview, Rebecca was bailed again despite further protests from Duncan that Rebecca could not be bailed unless she agreed and therefore she had to be charged or released. The sergeant followed his own law and bailed her regardless. 'Good God, these people are a law unto themselves,' worried Rebecca. She could see that Duncan was fighting hard for her. He really cared what happened but he was powerless. The police did whatever they wanted just like always.

Rebecca had been bailed for further investigations to take place. She was due to return a few months later. She had given the names of all the people that had given her money over the years including her parents, sister and close friends. She had given their contact details too. She knew that if the police spoke to them they could confirm what she had told them, not just about the money but also about her relationship with Raj. Rebecca pinned her hopes on the police making all the relevant enquiries. They were her lifeline.

Rebecca returned to work and continued to represent people in court. She knew some of the other lawyers were aware that she was being investigated but she stood strong and walked with her head held high. People were going to talk, that was human nature and that was exactly what the police wanted, but she was not going to let them destroy her. She had done nothing wrong. Rebecca was told that one of the dodgiest solicitors in the area had a special relationship with the CID investigating her. He had made remarks to Duncan on the day of her arrest. He hadn't told him directly but had made smart comments. The comments had gone over Duncan's head as he didn't realise the relevance to Rebecca at that time. The solicitor's connection to CID was an 'understanding' with officers that he was handed substantial cases to represent and in exchange he would give confidential information about his clients. Rebecca had been told by clients that he had taken drugs into prison for them and that he had helped them to make up defences for them. Despite this he found it a pleasure to bathe in her misery. He was jealous of Harters' success and saw Rebecca's as part of their team. Any fall by one of their members was satisfying for him. Rebecca wouldn't have been surprised if he had something to do with the police looking at her in the first place.

Rebecca tried to continue with her day to day life. She wasn't generally a worrier and when she felt things were getting on top of her she would just push them to the back of her mind. Only when she had a drink did she become hysterical. Her true fears were then out. Rebecca suffered more with physical signs of stress. She stopped having periods, suffered from a severe rash and had frequent migraines. These are all things that people who had never been in her position would not even contemplate or consider as an effect of being investigated. They just see the case in the papers during the trial or sentence. People don't really see the stress and worry that the person accused and their family have been through since the investigation first began. In some cases this can be years... and if someone is found not guilty there is no compensation for the mental torture that they have been through. The police attitude tends to be if you are found not guilty you have been lucky. You had 'got away with it' but if you are convicted, justice had been done.

CHAPTER THIRTEEN

Rebecca had had a terrible day at court... running around several different courtrooms representing each client as best she could. She didn't let her own case affect her work, she managed to put it all to one side and think about it as little as possible so that she could cope. She hadn't needed any time off, many people had told her that she would have been well within her rights to go to the doctors if she felt it was all too much but she wasn't going to let them win. She wasn't going to crumble. She didn't want to let Duncan down. Anyway, sitting at home feeling sorry for herself was not going to help the situation.

Rebecca had gone straight home after her cases had finished as it was too late to go back to the office. As she kicked off her shoes and fell back on to the sofa her phone rang. It was Duncan. 'Rebecca, are you on your own?' he asked softly. She instantly knew what was coming. She just had that feeling. That blow to the stomach when you feel physically sick. She had known it all along really. There was no way the police were going to admit they were wrong... They didn't think they were wrong. If they had taken the risk of arresting a solicitor they would never back down. She had tried to bury her instincts... that gut feeling that you should always listen to. She had ignored it from the beginning as dealing with the reality would have been too horrific.

'I'm so sorry,' offered Duncan, 'DS Rowley has just called. They are going to charge you. They want you at the police station next week.' Rebecca couldn't even respond. This was really going to happen. 'Look,' continued Duncan, 'take the rest of the week off and I'll meet you at the police station next week. We will deal with this. You have my support. Is there someone with you?' he repeated.

'Yes,' Rebecca managed to muster. Her throat was dry. She didn't want to worry Duncan. She coughed and hardened her voice. 'I'm fine,' she lied, 'I knew it was coming.'

'Do you want me to tell everyone at the office?'

'Yes please,' Rebecca answered gratefully.

There was a long pause... 'I am sorry,' said Duncan before he hung up. Rebecca knew he was genuinely sorry. He knew the whole case was absolute nonsense and that it had been built on the police's fantasy. He wasn't a man to show his feelings, he was strong and stern but he really cared about people and Rebecca knew this had upset him. She trusted him implicitly with her case. She had nothing to hide, she wanted him to see all the paperwork to reassure him that she was innocent. This wasn't really necessary. Anyone who knew her knew she hadn't done anything wrong... without question.

Rebecca put down the phone and called Anne. Her parents had pretty much moved down to the south since they knew of the allegations. They had even bought a new house so they could be near to give support. She told her mum what had happened. Within minutes her parents were there by her side. Rebecca couldn't believe how strong they were both being when she knew they must be crushed inside. They had been so proud of her and what she had achieved. They knew all too well that everything she had could be taken away from her... including her freedom. But this was their child... their baby, and people were trying to hurt her. The feelings of a protective parent override any other emotion and worry. They had to be Rebecca's strength. She couldn't cope with it alone.

She knew it would be in the press. The media would love this... 'Solicitor in drugs scandal.' That was the police's case, that she knew Raj had sold class A drugs and that she had tried to help him hide his drug money. Everyone would know all about it very soon. Real friends would be there, others would turn their back. People would talk, make things up and others who you would never have thought you could rely on would come through and be there.

The following week at the police station, Rebecca was quiet. DC Carter met her and Duncan at the door. She was still pretending to be Rebecca's best friend, chatting away like nothing was happening. Rebecca was just silent with no expression. She wasn't going to be nice but she didn't want them to see that they had affected her at all. She knew it was ridiculous but she wanted them to think she was taking all this in her stride. She was kidding herself.

DC Carter read the charges. 'Conspiracy to convert criminal property and conspiracy to disguise criminal property.' In a nutshell the case was that she had paid drugs money into her account to launder it for Raj and secondly, that she had tried to cover up and hide his drugs money by writing on the back of the letter from the Inland Revenue.

DC Carter had not contacted ANY of Rebecca's witnesses. Eight names and eight numbers had been given to her by Rebecca nearly six months ago and not one witness had been approached to confirm her account. Rebecca felt this was all part of the tactics... They wanted to charge Rebecca, they knew it would be covered heavily in the press and that her reputation would be forever in question. They did not want to hear the truth so they did not contact the witnesses. It was as simple as that.

'Raj Singh has been charged with drug offences and remanded,' DC Moran suddenly said out loud. All very blasé but clearly absolutely thrilled about it. Rebecca was shocked.

She felt a rush of panic for Raj followed by panic for herself. 'What the hell have they found to be able to charge and remand him? He isn't a prolific criminal or someone who would skip bail.' Rebecca pictured Raj's face with fear in his eyes. Rebecca felt inconsolable.

Rebecca was given a court date for the following week at the local magistrates' court. Rebecca dreaded the day. She knew there would be photographers waiting outside and that she would be the talk of the town. What an exciting scandal for everyone to talk about. But Rebecca wasn't going to break, she held her head high. She managed to convince her parents that they didn't need to come with her to court. 'Nothing will happen,' she told them, 'I'll just get another court date. It'll be a two minute hearing.' That was factually true but she also knew that there would be reporters and she would be in the dock. She wanted to prevent them seeing her like that for as long as possible.

Rebecca asked Marie to go with her. They went extra early to try and avoid people and especially the press. She didn't want to stand out so she dressed in a very non descript way and wore no make-up. Rebecca was usually so well groomed and took pride in her appearance. She didn't ever go out without making an effort. But today was different, she didn't want people to notice her. She didn't want to look like her.

In court, Duncan was given the paperwork confirming the prosecution case against her. There was no evidence included at all at this time, the documents consisted of the police's summary only. Rebecca heard her name called in the waiting room and stood up slowly, taking a deep breath as she did. Marie walked by her side to the courtroom. Rebecca was directed to the dock by the usher. This is so humiliating, she thought as she looked out at the clerk and magistrates and saw familiar faces that she had appeared in front of just weeks before.

Rebecca was given a court date for when she was to attend the Crown Court. This was when she would be joined with Raj and would have to face him. She learnt whilst at court that his family had been dragged into the case too. His sister, Suri, had already been charged months ago because she had £250,000 in her account that she accepted was his. She confirmed that she thought he was a car dealer and denied that she had any involvement or knowledge of drugs. That was obviously what Raj had alluded to previously when he said his sister had been arrested. She had never connected him to her arrest or thought it was anything to do with his money. Why would she? It wasn't a natural thought progression. Rebecca knew that Suri had been charged with something a couple of months before her arrest. Rebecca had been attending on one of her cases and had seen Suri Singh's name on the listing board. Surely not, she thought. That couldn't be Raj's sister could it?

As she walked up the steps to the courtroom she saw Raj sitting outside in the waiting area. 'Raj?' she called. 'Is everything OK?'

'Yeh,' he replied with not a care in the world, 'it's just my sister.'

Rebecca looked over to the corner of the area and saw Suri going into a consultation room with her barrister. She looked anxious and sad. 'What's going on?' she asked.

'Oh nothing, it's going to get thrown out today.' Rebecca had a million questions but she could tell by Raj's stance and inability to look at her that he didn't want to chat and wanted to get away.

'But what is she here for?' Rebecca pressed. 'Is she OK?'

Raj just played it down. 'It's getting sorted,' he told her.

Rebecca was none the wiser as she left to speak to her client. It played on her mind for the rest of the day but then was forgotten. 'He knows where I am if he needs me,' she told herself. She didn't want to involve herself in any drama unless she absolutely had to.

Weeks later, Raj text Rebecca to ask if he could come over to show her Suri's case papers. It must still be going then, Rebecca pondered. She replied that that was fine. She would happily give her advice on the evidence. Raj didn't text her later. He didn't bring the papers over. Rebecca still did not know what was going on.

Back in court, the court papers showed that the house that Raj had been living in had apparently been purchased with a deposit from him and had a mortgage for the remainder. The mortgage had been in his sister and mother's name but had been paid by him. His mother had been charged with money laundering for getting the mortgage on Raj's behalf.

Raj's father had been charged with paying a small amount of money into his account that had come from Raj. It was alleged that the whole family knew that his money was dirty money from drugs. It was all a complete mess. Whatever Raj had been up to it seemed that anyone with a connection to him had been dragged into it. The whole family maintained that Raj was a car trader and so did Raj himself. Rebecca's case would join with the others at the next court hearing. She had never had anything to do with his family. There had been a couple of years of hiding the relationship, picking up Raj from the corner of his street and not being able to go around to his house. Raj's family had finally confronted Raj about him having a girlfriend and he had reluctantly told them about Rebecca. Following his admission, Rebecca had seen them in passing but had never been involved in any family things. They did not have a relationship. Rebecca knew that this was because of cultural differences. They accepted that Raj was with a white girl for the time being but hoped that he would have an arranged marriage or meet someone from his own religion and his own caste and that Rebecca was just a passing phase.

His brother, Gilly, had serious alcohol and drugs problems. He was a loose cannon. Rebecca had seen him around from time to time but had never had anything to do with him. Raj never told Rebecca anything about his brother. All his discussions over the phone with his family were in Punjabi and she couldn't understand any of what was being said. She had gathered that they had a poor relationship. She could see that Raj was embarrassed of his brother and the shame he had brought on his family by being an addict. But his brother, Gilly, respected Raj no matter what. It was, again, a cultural thing. Raj was the older brother and was therefore, almost, in charge of the family. No matter what he did no one questioned, no one ever answered him back and there was no affection between any of them. Gilly was dangerous, not in a macho, tough way but in an unpredictable, irrational way. He had nothing to lose and would do anything to impress or please his big brother.

From the prosecution summary Rebecca had learnt that Gilly had gone to court at one of Raj's first bail hearings. He had shouted out at the judge that he was the culprit. He had sworn at the judge and had been arrested for contempt of court. When he was searched, a receipt had been found in his pocket. It was for a Fiat Uno that had been sold for £5000. He was trying to help Raj by manufacturing paperwork to back up his car trade. This was typical of Gilly, he was making things much worse for everyone. He was probably pleased that he was actually included in the case and that he had proved to his big brother that he was willing to try and help.

Early one Sunday morning, Rebecca was in bed when she heard a banging on the door. She looked out and saw Gilly standing there. She didn't want to answer but he kept banging and banging. It didn't seem that he would ever give up. Rebecca was worried about him waking the neighbours and causing a scene. She went down and answered the door...

'What have you said about my brother?' Gilly slurred aggressively.

'What?' Rebecca answered, she was aware that Gilly could be violent. She was frightened to shut the door in case it angered him and he pushed it open to attack her; he was much stronger than her, he could easily force his way in. She knew she just had to pacify him until he calmed down and went away. 'I don't know what you mean,' Rebecca told him. 'I haven't said anything. I just told the police what I knew.'

Gilly seemed to calm slightly. 'Right, well, I'll ring you when I've spoken to Raj. Give me your number,' he demanded.

Rebecca had to think quick, she did not want to be dragged into Gilly's plan. 'I don't know my number off by heart,' she claimed... 'it's new. You give me yours and I'll ring you,' she promised.

She wrote Gilly's number down and shut the door behind him, double locking it. She was relieved he had gone. She was still worried that the police were watching her. She had become more and more paranoid. What if they saw Gilly at the door and tried to make something out of it? She called Duncan.

'That's witness intimidation,' he said, 'my advice is to call the police.' Rebecca didn't want to. She felt that Gilly was the lesser of those two evils.

'I'll call them if he comes round again,' she promised Duncan.

Weeks passed when a letter with familiar writing landed on Rebecca's porch floor. It was from Raj.

'I'm so sorry you have been dragged into this. I know Gilly came round and scared you. I have told him to stay away from you. You don't deserve any of this. You have done nothing wrong. I promise I won't let anything happen to you, not you or my family'.

Rebecca showed Duncan the letter. 'The police will just say he wrote it to try and protect you.' He shrugged. Rebecca didn't reply to the letter... she had so many questions for Raj. She didn't know what was going on herself but she was aware that whatever she did could be used her against her. She couldn't risk that.

Just as Rebecca thought it couldn't get any worse a letter from the bank was delivered.

'We have reviewed your account and your overdraft will be removed in 28 days.'

'28 days!' Rebecca was in shock. This was the bank that the police had contacted to access her accounts. They were obviously aware of what was going on. 'They can't do this!' Rebecca told herself. They could. They weren't saying it was because of the case. They simply said they had reviewed her account. She hadn't been running her account any differently than normal. She had a huge overdraft that she had run up while she studied. She basically lived in her overdraft. If her next pay went into the account it would be swallowed up without the overdraft. 'Not exactly innocent until proven guilty.' Rebecca sighed.

She had to start using an alternative bank account while she made arrangements to clear her overdraft on a monthly basis. She didn't need this extra stress. The police had not put a restraint on her account. They apparently believed a huge amount of money had been paid into her account but they didn't try to seize it. Rebecca thought that was very telling. The bank had obviously jumped to their own conclusions. Rebecca had already been tried and convicted by them.

CHAPTER FOURTEEN

Rebecca had again managed to persuade her parents and her friends that they did not need to come to the first hearing at the Crown Court... 'It's OK, honestly,' she told them. 'It will just be fixing a date for the trial. We will be in and out in minutes. It's no big deal,' she assured them. Marie was going to go with Rebecca. They were meeting Duncan there. They had chosen a barrister. He was someone Rebecca had met through work. He had defended some of her own clients. She had been impressed with him and his depth of knowledge. She had liked him immediately on meeting him. His name was Matthew Williams... Rebecca felt confident that he could fight her corner and she put her trust in him.

Once again they got there early to avoid any photographers and journalists that may be waiting outside to get their scoop. Rebecca breathed a sigh of relief when she saw no one was waiting outside for her. It was a weight off her mind to know she would not be in the next edition of the local paper.

Once inside, Rebecca saw Raj's family across the foyer. They caught each other's eyes but didn't even acknowledge each other. After a while Suri came across and gave Rebecca a letter that Raj had written to them. Rebecca read the letter as Suri walked back over to her family. It was an apology to his family for what they were going through. He admitted in the letter that he hadn't been paying tax and had been clocking cars for years so that he could make extra money on them. He admitted that he had broken the law but maintained that he had never sold or had anything to do with drugs. 'My barrister told me to show this to you so that you can show your legal team,' Suri had told her. That was the end of their conversation. Rebecca showed Matthew and Duncan the letter. 'This won't make any difference,' said Duncan.

'They will just say he's trying to cover his tracks,' Matthew agreed. Raj couldn't do anything now to save Rebecca. If he told them the truth they would just say he was lying to save her. She couldn't win.

Rebecca knew that today would be a very quick hearing. She had attended plea hearings hundreds of times and had even conducted them herself. It was probably her familiarity with the process that saved her sanity. She wasn't afraid because it wasn't the unknown. The pleas would be taken, dates would be set for paperwork to be served and a trial date would be set for when a jury would finally decide everyone's verdict.

Rebecca had already discussed her plea with Peter and Duncan. There was no question, she was innocent. She had not taken any money from Raj and she wasn't trying to help him hide drugs money by writing on the back of that letter. She was not guilty. She was going to prove her innocence. She had no idea what everyone else was going to plead. She had kept herself completely separate from the other defendants. The prosecution would have loved to see any sort of relationship between them. They would have used it to claim it was all a conspiracy and show a tight bond between them all. Rebecca had to think about her every action whilst the investigation was ongoing.

While she was outside the courtroom Rebecca saw a reporter. He did not seem interested in Rebecca at all and was just scanning through the court listings on the screen outside. Rebecca watched as DC Carter boldly walked up to the reporter and spoke to him. She saw her point over to Rebecca and continue her discussions. The reporter could not keep his eyes off Rebecca. He got straight on his phone and kept Rebecca within his sights. She knew what was coming. The photographers would be waiting outside.

Rebecca spoke to Duncan about her concerns. She knew that there was nothing that could be done. There were no grounds for any restrictions to be put on reporting. 'There's nothing we can do, you know that yourself,' he told her sadly.

In court, Rebecca saw the two barristers that would be prosecuting. Jason Cassidy and Christopher Kallow. Cassidy was the principle barrister who led the case. Rebecca despised him at first sight. He was a little smarmy man who did not try to hide that he was enjoying every moment of her misery. Kallow was simply Cassidy's sidekick. Both equally as arrogant as each other, they gave Rebecca a chill every time they slithered past her.

Six of them stood in the dock. The security guards and interpreters squeezed in. Rebecca heard the keys jangling and the locks being turned. She knew Raj was being brought up from the cells and her stomach turned over.

In the dock, Rebecca saw Raj for the first time in over a year. He made no eye contact with her at all. They could have been strangers. If the prosecution were right about him, he was a stranger, Rebecca had not known him at all. Rebecca was stood the furthest away from Raj. They didn't communicate. She didn't know how she felt about that.

In turn each of the defendants entered a not guilty plea to every charge put to them. Raj denied the drugs charges and all the money laundering charges connected to Rebecca and his family. There were sixteen counts on the indictment altogether. This was a huge case. Rebecca was worried that her part would become lost during all the information that the jury were to be given. She was concerned that she would just be swept along with everyone else. What if the jury could not focus on the evidence for and against her and would be overwhelmed with the amount of information given?

The trial date was set for December. It was expected to take two months. Rebecca had four more months of waiting.

She had to prepare and be ready. She knew her life better than anyone. The life that the prosecution were claiming was hers was a lie.

Rebecca and Marie waited in the court foyer. 'Have they gone?' Rebecca asked her sister.

Marie looked out of the door at the photographers lurking outside. 'No.'

'They won't leave.' Rebecca knew it. They had already waited for two hours. What were the options? ...swap clothes with Marie? They'd still recognise her and might put in their article that she was trying to hide... Run? They would photograph her running and that would make her look guilty... 'Let's just leave with a group.' Rebecca knew that she should just hold her head up high but the thought of a photo of her in the paper being vilified by the press was something she could do without. She knew that people wouldn't question if she was innocent or not. They would believe what they read. The press rarely print the defendant's version of events. It wasn't an interesting read to hear that someone had done nothing wrong. If she could avoid it she would. They left with a group of people... but were spotted by the reporter who had been tipped off by DC Carter. The photographer ran after Rebecca up the street. She couldn't run. She scurried into a pub to escape.

'Give her a break.' Marie scowled at the photographer as he stood outside the door waiting for Rebecca to leave.

'Is there a back door? Rebecca asked the bar staff desperately.

'No, I'm sorry there's not,' was the reply. The lady looked genuinely sorry for Rebecca. She could see that she was close to tears. Rebecca was trapped. Rebecca waited for over an hour but she realised that she had no option but to walk out of the pub and let them get the shot they wanted. She took a deep breath and walked out. He was waiting. He sprinted in front of Rebecca to get the best possible picture. She was powerless. She just had to let him.

Sure enough the next edition of the local paper had a huge front page picture of Rebecca with the headline... 'Local Solicitor in Drugs Scandal'.... Rebecca didn't cry. It was out of her control. She had had time to get used to the idea and she knew it was coming.

Rebecca's friends started to ring as they woke up to the headline... most were in tears. 'Why are they doing this to you? You don't deserve this,' they cried. Texts came pouring in from people who had just found out what had been going on... 'No one believes any of that shit in the papers.' 'We are behind you 100%.' Rebecca knew she had good friends who would support her. Now she was going to have to ask for a much more demanding type of support from each of them which would test their friendships to the limit.

CHAPTER FIFTEEN

Rebecca's close friendship group had known what was going on from the very beginning... right from her arrest. She trusted them all completely and knew that it would not go any further.

Part of Rebecca's defence was firstly, that she hadn't taken any money from Raj and secondly, that her relationship with Raj was not as the police had claimed. It was nowhere near as close as they believed. The police thought that Rebecca was trying to distance herself from Raj but she was in fact just telling them exactly how it had been. Their relationship was dysfunctional. It was not normal and that was exactly why Rebecca had got out of it in the end. Her friends knew this, they had been around at the time, they knew how upset Rebecca used to be and how unstable they had been as a couple. She needed her friends to stand up in court and tell the judge and jury what they knew. Each of her friends could state, under oath, that Rebecca had also been the organiser of social events and that she had lent a lot of them money when they needed it. She had even paid for Nicola to go on holiday. Nicola had repaid her in dribs and drabs over the next year. Rebecca had paid that money, in cash, into her account

Rebecca asked her friends if they would be prepared to go and be a witness for her. She knew it was a lot to ask. So many people would be frightened at just the prospect of having to go to court. 'Of course I will,' said Nicola. 'Just tell me when I need to be there,' promised Annette. 'No problem at all,' assured Marie. Not one of her friends hesitated. They knew she needed them. Rebecca was so grateful to have such a supportive and reliable group of friends. She loved them all.

Rebecca needed her parents to give evidence too. They needed to confirm that they had given money to Rebecca, in cash, consistently through the years. They also could say what they knew of her relationship with Raj... not much would be the answer. He had never bothered or made any effort with her family. He had never got to know them. He had been separate from her family just as she had been with his.

Everyone made Rebecca feel that she could depend on them. They made her feel that nothing was too much for them. They were prepared to stand up for Rebecca and support her through it all. All the support made Rebecca feel so lucky.

Duncan took statements from each of Rebecca's witnesses. There were seven in all. Each of them said the same thing over and over again. It was exactly the same as Rebecca had said in interview.

The full prosecution case papers came through... late, just as they had expected. Duncan and Matthew set about preparing the defence. They were served with the interviews of all the defendants including Raj. Rebecca read through it all. He had never been asked about Rebecca. He hadn't made any comment in any of his interviews. The police had never put to him if Rebecca had had any involvement in anything. He hadn't been given any opportunity to deny or confirm her involvement.

Raj's family had been asked about Rebecca and confirmed that they knew she was Raj's girlfriend quite some time ago. They did not know any more about her. Suri did not even know Rebecca's last name.

It was clear from the case papers that the prosecution were going to take the angle that Rebecca had full knowledge of Raj's drug dealing and that she was complicit in it. She had knowingly helped him and that was how he had managed to get away with it for so many years. She was painted as a gangster's moll who was manipulative and conniving. Just like the press, they had vilified her.

The prosecution had decided to go for a charge of money laundering rather that perverting the course of justice which was what Rebecca was initially arrested for. This meant that despite running the case at its highest and claiming that Rebecca knew about all the dodgy dealing, in fact they only had to prove that she was suspicious of something criminal, not drugs. How do you prove you are not suspicious? Rebecca thought.

The change in charge almost reversed the burden of proof. It lowered the standard... proving someone was suspicious is a lot easier than proving someone knew something. Rebecca was aware that the police were charging these cases often rather than charging a handling stolen goods case as they had less to prove for a conviction. They were getting better statistics this way and looked like they were doing a better job.

It was all out in the open now and everyone knew. Most colleagues from the local court were supportive of Rebecca. She received cards and messages each telling her that they knew the whole thing was rubbish.

The only negativity she saw was from the prosecutors... particularly the women. Bitchy comments and gossiping were rife. Rebecca just ignored them. The people who made them did not know her. She expected it from a couple of the older women. They had always been off with younger, new solicitors and were extremely aggressive and pro prosecution... they wanted convictions at all costs. They were completely wrong for the jobs they were in but unfortunately were the exact type of people that the role attracted.

A female defence solicitor that had gone to university with Rebecca started spreading rumours to the other solicitors at court. Despite always getting on well with Rebecca, she told everyone that at university Rebecca had always boasted about Raj and told everyone that he had given her lots of money. This was a complete lie... there was no reason for her to make this up and so Rebecca could not understand why she would say it.

She needed all the support she could get and was having the most traumatic and testing period of her life but this woman took pleasure in kicking her while she was down. Rebecca had hardly known the woman at university and would never have spoken to the girl about any relationship she was in but, more importantly, she hadn't even met Raj until after university. The prosecution accepted that they had not met until late 2001-early 2002. Rebecca had left university in summer 2001.

Duncan must have heard the rumours but didn't even ask Rebecca about it... he was furious. He knew the solicitor was trying to cast doubt on Rebecca's character and tarnish her reputation further. He did not want to give her the pleasure of a response. Rebecca learnt a very important lesson... sometimes people just do nasty things for no obvious reason... There would be others out there who would be envious and jealous of her... they would relish the opportunity to stick the boot in when she was down. People who had never known Rebecca turned their backs all around her. Those who used to smile and politely chat now turned away so they didn't catch her eye.

During the wait for trial, Rebecca would try and continue her life as she had done before. She would still socialise regularly with friends and more often than not would be out on the town on a Saturday night. Rebecca found herself drinking more and more on each occasion to escape from her reality. She found it helped at first but the drunker she got the more hysterical she felt about her situation.

There were several occasions when she would run from her friends in tears, make-up down her face, and not answer the phone to them for hours. Annette and Jennifer where worried sick. They knew she was on the edge and was controlling it well while sober. Her anxiety took over when she was drunk.

Rebecca had gone out with Marie and Jennifer one night. Rebecca walked into the toilets and heard the others talking about giving evidence. She felt betrayed that they were discussing her behind her back. She selfishly did not give a thought to how the case was making everyone else feel. They had all had a drink and emotions were running high. 'Don't talk about me!' Rebecca yelled aggressively at her sister.

'We are talking about it coz we are scared,' Marie replied. 'We didn't want to worry you with it.' Rebecca was completely irrational and immediately felt that everyone was against her. She couldn't see that Marie was trying to stay strong for her and was confiding her own fears to Jennifer as she was in the same boat.

'Don't come to court then!' Rebecca screeched. 'I don't need you. I don't need anyone.' She gulped back her tears. 'I'll do this on my own.' Rebecca ran out of the club and on to the street.

Rebecca disappeared sobbing and decided to go and think about things at the embankment. As Rebecca sat on the side of the river she pushed herself close to the edge and for a split second she considered jumping in. At that moment Rebecca realised that she could not drink whilst the case was going on. She just did not trust herself. She did not recognise the person she became. She was like a lunatic, wandering around on her own, hysterically. She needed to take control back.

CHAPTER SIXTEEN

The day had arrived. The first day of trial. Rebecca had just tried to put it to the back of her mind until she had to deal with it. She had carried on as before, going to work and socialising as always. Now was the day that she would have to deal with it, she couldn't ignore it any longer. She was staying with Anne and Peter. The two people she could always rely on. The two that would support her no matter what. They had been so strong and shown no signs of cracking but Rebecca knew it must be killing them inside. They remained positive. They were determined to get her through this.

A forensic accountants report had been prepared. It had considered the withdrawals from Peter and Anne's account and the deposits into Rebecca's account. The report concluded that there were vague but consistent patterns connecting the two accounts. The trouble was that Rebecca hadn't always paid her parents' money straight into her account. Sometimes there were days when she could not get to the bank, or times when she spent half of the money given in cash and only paid in part of it. It was so hard to cross reference everything, especially as it had gone back years and years. The important part though was that the withdrawals from her parents' account covered more than the money she had paid in. Surely this must count for something, she hoped.

The three arrived at court. Rebecca looked out for photographers as she approached the building. Another photo was the last thing she needed right now. As soon as she entered the building she saw Raj's family. They all looked up and smiled nervously. They knew she was there for nothing and the guilt they felt for that was written all over their faces.

Each individual defendant had a separate barrister. The prosecution still had their two. A senior barrister and a junior. Both equally as unlikeable as each other. They swooped through court with not a care in the world. They had no feelings as to what they were about to try and do. There were six defendants in all. Raj, his parents, his brother Gilly, his sister Suri and Rebecca. The case had all started with just Suri. Now everyone was in the dock with her.

There were discussions before the case began between the barristers. Desperate agreements were trying to be reached to avoid a trial and ultimately avoid convictions.

Rebecca and her legal team were not party to the talks. 'No matter what, there will be a trial for one defendant...' the senior prosecutor, Mr Kallow, announced to the judge. Rebecca knew that meant her. They weren't going to stop... no matter what. They had a point to prove and they had gone too far to admit they were wrong.

Rebecca sat with her parents in the café at the court waiting for the hearing to start. She saw her name flash up on the listing screen... it was surreal. She still couldn't believe it was real. She was living it but not registering it.

'All parties in the case of Singh and others to Court 1 please.' This was it... they were being called in.

Anne and Peter had to wait outside the courtroom so that they could give evidence in the defence of Rebecca later in the trial. Siobhan and Martin, Rebecca's auntie and uncle had travelled down from the north to be there with her. Her family had been amazing. They had divided all their time to be able to attend so that she was never in court on her own. They had to travel from all over the country for hours at a time to be there. They completely had to put their lives on hold while they all looked after Rebecca.

Rebecca walked to the back of the court where the dock was opened by a guard. She was led behind a glass screen. Raj's family followed and they all sat in a row with the interpreters splitting. There was no conversation. Rebecca just stared straight ahead. She pulled out her Rosary beads that Jennifer had bought her. They were a great comfort for her. They made her feel safe. She prayed silently over and over, clutching the beads tightly. She heard keys jangling, then being turned in a lock. She knew Raj was being brought in. She didn't know how she felt about seeing him. She just kept looking forward. Raj's family were talking in Punjabi to him... Rebecca couldn't understand what was being said but she could hear from their tones that they were pleased to see him. They were talking as if they were all on a day trip out not sat in a Crown Court dock together. Rebecca didn't get involved she just carried on looking straight ahead.

Everyone stood as the judge entered. Rebecca had seen him before when she had pleaded not guilty. He reminded her of a tortoise. He was an elderly gentleman, with a full head of grey hair and small ageing features. He walked slowly to his bench and bowed towards the courtroom.

Mr Kallow opened the discussions. 'It has been agreed that no evidence is to be offered on all counts against Suri Singh. Ms Singh does, however, agree to sign over the money that was frozen in her bank accounts.'

Rebecca couldn't believe it. They had all made a plea bargain.

He continued... 'Mrs Singh will be pleading guilty as will Mr Singh and Gilly Singh. Raj Singh will be entering pleas to the money laundering counts but maintains his not guilty pleas on the drugs charges.'

Raj's parents had to accept that they had paid money into their bank accounts on behalf of Raj. Mrs Singh accepted that she had got a mortgage on behalf of Raj. Gilly agreed that he had tried to make up receipts after Raj had been arrested to help cover up for Raj.

Suri was to walk free. It was all over for her. Rebecca was pleased for her. She had been through hell. She had been wrapped up in this for years. You could see on her face it had taken its toll. She was painfully thin and her skin was almost grey.

A small part of Rebecca felt resentful that they were walking away seemingly unscathed and she was still stuck in the nightmare. Suri had paid nearly quarter of a million pounds into her bank account for Raj, yet she was free. Rebecca knew the only reason she was standing there was because she was a solicitor. They had her in their grasp and there was no way they were going to let her go without a fight.

Because Rebecca was a solicitor, there was a higher level of expectation on her. She was to behave in a certain way and anything below that was punishable. What do I benefit from such a position? Rebecca often thought. She was still human. She wasn't paid a particularly good wage, wasn't treated any differently in everyday life, what's the point? I'd rather just work in the local supermarket or down the pub and not worry. Rebecca had seriously contemplated this on a regular basis.

The trial was to continue for Rebecca and Raj. Raj for his drug charges and Rebecca for supposedly paying in Raj's cash and writing his car expenses down for him.

The sentences for the family were adjourned until the end of the trial. The dock door was opened and they were all led out. It just left the two.

During preparations for the trial, Duncan had had several consultations with Rebecca to take a statement from her and go through the ins and outs of her relationship with Raj. This was so embarrassing for Rebecca. She was telling her boss the fine details of her personal life and her finances, including a large amount of debt, were spread out for him to see.

Duncan never made Rebecca feel embarrassed. He never commented or passed judgement as she told him how Raj had treated her and made her feel. Duncan asked Rebecca if Raj had ever hit her. 'Just once.' When she heard it out loud she knew how it sounded. 'Just once? Just?' Rebecca described how her and Raj were not together at the time. He had sent his friend to Rebecca's to pick up some of his property while he waited in the car.

'I'll go and sort it out,' Rebecca had told the friend as she shut the front door. She then started gathering Raj's bits to pass outside.

The next thing Rebecca knew Raj was banging on the door demanding his stuff. Rebecca opened the door wondering why he was so angry. She had told his friend that she was getting it. She was doing what he had asked. Raj stormed in ranting about how he wanted his things now and Rebecca shouted back walking towards him. The next thing Rebecca remembered was lying on her bed holding her lip. 'Get out!' she screamed at him as he just looked at her in shock. She could see in his face he could not quite believe what he had done. They had had hundreds of arguments over the years, and most were a lot more heated and serious than that day, but Raj had never raised a hand to her before. He left without saying a word. Rebecca looked in the mirror and saw that her lip was cut and bleeding. It had swollen up where her tooth had chipped and cut into her lip. She looked a mess. It wasn't something that she could cover up but she didn't want anyone to know. She felt embarrassed and, strangely, didn't want anyone to know Raj had done that in case they didn't like him because of it.

She told Marie she had been hit in the face with a cricket ball whilst walking through the park. Marie was suspicious but she had no choice but to accept what Rebecca said.

Later that night, Rebecca heard a knock at the door. She opened it and flinched when she saw Raj standing there. He was visibly upset at the sight of her. She could see the tears welling in his eyes. 'I'm sorry,' he pleaded,' but you wouldn't give me my stuff.' He was still trying to justify it and blame Rebecca in some way. Rebecca listened to his half-hearted apology and asked him to leave. They did get back together some months later just as always.

Duncan made a note of what Rebecca was saying without a reaction. She was ready to justify Raj's behaviour and justify her response but she didn't need to.

Now that Suri was not a defendant she potentially helped Rebecca's case. She had Raj's money in her bank account and the case had been dropped against her. She lived with Raj, she was his sister and yet she was adamant that he had nothing to do with drugs and that she knew nothing about it. She too described Raj as a car trader and thought that that was where his money came from. If she didn't know then how could Rebecca? That was a strong support for Rebecca. She needed Suri to give evidence. They did not have a relationship for Rebecca to ask Suri. Matthew and Duncan approached Suri's barrister and asked if they would ask her to consider it.

'It's the least she can do after what her brother has done,' Anne snapped. Rebecca knew that Suri would be reluctant. She had been going through this for years and it had only just finished for her. Rebecca hoped that she could see how much she needed her and that she would have the heart to help.

Suri said no. She could not go through giving evidence. Rebecca was gutted. How can she not help? she thought. She knows it's the right thing to do.

CHAPTER SEVENTEEN

The next day Rebecca arrived at court with her parents, auntie and uncle. The previous day had exhausted them all even though nothing much had happened.

The court hearing started on time. There was no waiting around. The preliminary matters had been dealt with now. It was time for the jury to be sworn in.

Rebecca sat in the dock behind the glass next to Raj. They still hadn't spoken. They hadn't even made eye contact. They watched as the eligible jurors stood in the corner of the court waiting for their names to be called. Each of them peered through the glass at Rebecca, not wanting to appear obvious but desperate to look at what was behind. Rebecca felt like she was a zoo animal. People looking at her, staring, judging. People who didn't know her and would never really get to know the real her.

As the jury was selected they each took a place on one of the twelve seats until they were all finally full. The remaining people were sent away. Seven women and five men... Rebecca wasn't sure if that was good or bad. She generally got on with both men and women. Women could be bitchy, but then men aren't as emotional and are unlikely to empathise with Rebecca. She was driving herself mad analysing what the jury might be thinking. She was scared... these strangers were there to decide her fate. She glanced across at the one person who was feeling exactly the same as her. She caught Raj's eye for the first time and could tell he was thinking the same.

Mr Kallow opened the prosecution case. Rebecca should have been prepared for what was about to come. She was a solicitor and had heard it all before... but she was shocked. She could not believe the fanciful story that was told. Kallow told Rebecca's life as if he had lived it but it was all wrong. It was what they thought had happened being told as if it actually had.

According to Kallow, Rebecca was a manipulative monster. Raj had been a major player in the drugs world and he had only got away with it for so long because of her. She was the mastermind behind the business and had helped Raj to cover his tracks as he peddled death. She was described as Raj's, 'lover, lawyer and financial advisor'. Kallow was so theatrical in his presentation, gesturing and pointing towards Rebecca to emphasize his most derogatory points.

Rebecca shook her head as she listened. She looked over to the public gallery and saw her family listening to the awful things being said about her. She shouldn't have been so shocked but when you know the things being said about you are complete lies the temptation is to jump up and defend yourself... but that was the worst thing that she could have done. She had to think about how the jury would view her. They glanced over during the speech... looking at the despicable animal being described.

Finally it came to an end. Kallow had made it so believable, she could have even doubted herself. She was worried... what if the jury believed him?

Duncan's son, Ryan had been sitting behind Matthew, making notes and assisting him with getting the many papers in order. Ryan knew Rebecca from work. During the lunch break Ryan approached Rebecca. 'I didn't like that,' he told her, upset. 'I didn't like him saying those things about you. They aren't true. You're not like that at all.'

'I know,' she reassured him. 'It's OK, we will get our chance to show the jury what I'm really like.' She smiled but inside she wasn't quite as sure it would be so easy.

As the trial continued, the prosecution called their witnesses to prove Rebecca and Raj's guilt. Rebecca's family members relentlessly travelled up and down the country to support her and make sure she was never alone in the court. Her friends that were not giving evidence took time off work to show their support. There were constantly people in the public gallery in Rebecca's corner. She couldn't have carried on without them, she was so grateful.

Raj didn't really have any support throughout the trial. On one occasion, his mother came into the gallery. She didn't understand what was being said due to the language barrier and so was more of a distraction than a support. She went in and out of the court disturbing others as she went past. As she sat there, she often opened sweets and offered them around to Rebecca's horrified family. Her phone was kept switched on, it interrupted proceedings several times as people called for updates. Rebecca felt sorry for Raj. He was on his own.

Raj had two barristers because his charges were so serious. He had a senior advocate, Mr Martin, and junior counsel, Ginger, who assisted in the preparation. Raj and Rebecca were often given paperwork to refer to. They had to share what was given to them and so the odd word started to be exchanged. Rebecca was slowly starting to feel closer to him.

Kallow made an application for the previous convictions of some of Raj's associates to be admitted. The first was of a man who had been convicted of drug dealing and who had been in the car with Rebecca and Jennifer that time the police had stopped them for a routine check. Certainly no drugs had been found at the time and he wasn't convicted of the offence until years later but the prosecution asserted that it was guilt by association. Rebecca didn't even know who this man was. He was driving the car for the few minutes that she was in it.

She knew nothing about him and it hadn't occurred to her to ask.

Secondly, a phone that was found at Raj's address was registered to a known drug user. The suggestion was that he had given Raj his phone as he owed him money. Raj's defence asserted that it was a phone he had purchased. The mere presence of the phone was the evidence. Rebecca had never heard of or seen the drug user before. She had no connection to him at all. 'Who the hell is this person?' She sighed.

The judge agreed to admit the previous convictions to show the connection to Raj and drugs. Ginger scurried to the back of court. Rebecca heard her tell Raj that this decision was wrong in law and could later be grounds for appeal. Raj nodded.

At the end of the second day, the evidence had been about Raj and the searches at his house. They didn't concern Rebecca directly. As the court was adjourned for the day Raj's junior counsel, Ginger, asked to speak to the judge without the jury being present.

Rebecca listened. Ginger told the judge that the case had been in the national papers. She named three papers with coverage and showed the judge a photo of Rebecca printed in the middle of the story. The article was all about Rebecca. Raj did not feature heavily. Rebecca again was made out to be a devious monster. Rebecca did not realise there had been such national coverage. She put her head down and broke down. National humiliation with a photograph just to make sure. She couldn't believe this was happening. Rebecca knew Peter would have seen the photo that morning as that was the paper he was reading before court. He had chosen not to tell her to save her upset. As tears streamed down her face, she continued to look down to hide her distress. She did not want the prosecution to have the pleasure. She was sure they would be delighted at having a publicised case. That would definitely boost their profile.

Rebecca felt a hand on top of hers as she sobbed silently. The hand squeezed hers. It was Raj. 'Please don't cry,' he told her. 'It'll be OK.' Court had adjourned and he was pulled away by the guards and taken back into the cells. Rebecca looked up and saw tears in his eyes as the door closed. She had been thrown into a situation where he was the only person in the world who could understand how she was feeling and who was feeling exactly the same.

Rebecca had been warned not to talk to Raj as if the jury saw they would believe the prosecution's assertion that they were in it together and were 'thick as thieves'. In truth, Rebecca hadn't been close to Raj for years but ironically this situation was pushing them closer together. It was like a game. No one could show how they really felt. Rebecca couldn't be seen to be communicating with Raj. She had to act like he wasn't there. Why couldn't the jury just see that they were just two people trying to lean on each other? The prosecution would use it if they even saw a flicker of affection between the two of them. They had to be wary.

At the end of the day those that had come to support couldn't believe how things happened in court. For those with no experience of the court system it was shocking to hear things being told to the jury that they knew not to be the truth. The sense of injustice flowed through family and friends. Everyone wanted to be at court as much as possible. People were surprised at how involved and incensed they felt about the case after coming for just a few hours. More and more people came and more and more people kept coming.

Not all of Rebecca's closest friends were supportive. One of Rebecca's oldest school friends was Louise. Louise had practically lived at Rebecca's house all through university and school years. They spent most days together and were extremely close. Louise knew all about the case and had been vocally outraged by it all. 'I'll be there tomorrow,' she assured Rebecca. The next day Louise was nowhere to be seen. Rebecca received a text, 'so sorry, couldn't get out of work. I'll def come tomorrow.'

'Poor Louise,' Rebecca said to Anne and Peter. 'She's really trying but can't seem to get there.' Anne and Peter said nothing but exchanged glances.

Louise worked for the family business so Rebecca assumed that they were being difficult with Louise taking a day off. She knew from previous experiences that they could be demanding on Louise at times so Rebecca believed her excuse and accepted it.

It wasn't until days later when Louise still hadn't turned up to court and Rebecca was telling Anne that she felt sorry for Louise that the truth came out. 'You need to know the truth,' Anne suddenly snapped. 'Louise has told Marie that she did not want to come to court in case it jeopardises her police application.'

Rebecca had forgotten that Louise had been trying to get into the police. She knew that there was an ongoing application but it did not cross her mind for a second that Louise wouldn't support her because of it.

Rebecca was shocked and upset. 'I just can't stand her lying to you, sending you texts everyday saying she's sorry she's not made it yet,' Anne blurted out. 'That girl was at our house day in day out for years and she can't even support you when you're going through hell.' Anne was visibly upset.

Rebecca made the decision there and then to cut Louise off. She needed real friends right now and had no time for those she couldn't rely on.

Rebecca never spoke to Louise again. A tear stained letter from Louise was dropped through her door. She explained that the minute she said her fears out loud to Marie she regretted them. She apologised and asked Rebecca to ring her but it was too late. Rebecca could never forgive her. She felt too let down.

CHAPTER EIGHTEEN

While Peter and Anne waited outside the courtroom, they mixed with people whom they would have never normally crossed paths with. There seemed a general sense of unity amongst those waiting for verdicts. They all knew what the other was feeling. There was real sympathy and genuine empathy.

In particular, Anne began talking to the young boy whose case was being heard in the courtroom next door. He was tall and very slim. His skin was pale, as if it had never seen daylight. Anne learnt from the young man that he was on trial for murder. He had been released on appeal after serving eight years in prison and was now being retried for the same crime.

Anne told Peter, 'I have spoken to Robert for thirty minutes and there is nothing more certain than his innocence.'

He had previously been convicted on the basis of expert evidence which had found particles on his clothing. The expert in his original trial testified that these could have only come from contact with the murdered body. Over the years other experts ascertained that the particles can, in fact, come from a number of things including flicking a lighter. Robert was a smoker as were many people that he could have been around the night of the murder. Apart from that evidence, there was no connection from Robert to the murder. The prosecution was based solely on the story concocted by the police around their flawed expert evidence. Anne prayed that this jury could see that.

Days later Anne was sitting with Peter outside court lost in thought when the court door came flying open and Robert came flying out. Oh God, she thought, he's making a run for it.

Robert ran straight over to Anne and flung his arms around her. 'Not Guilty!' he screeched. 'It's over, it's over!' Anne felt exhilarated. She had formed quite a bond with Robert over the past weeks and she was so happy that his name had been cleared.

Years later, Anne read that another man had been linked through DNA evidence to the body and that he had been convicted. Rebecca had been told that up until the DNA had been found the police were still focussing on Robert as the culprit and although he had been cleared by the court, he still had their watchful eyes over him.

In Court 2, Rebecca watched as the prosecution evidence against her was called. The evidence was completely financial. It was about her bank accounts and that piece of paper she had written on. The only evidence of her relationship with Raj was from Rebecca herself. Should she have kept her mouth shut in interview? She had not tried to hide anything. She told the police about their relationship and described how on and off it was. They accused her of trying to distance herself and not being truthful about it. They had no evidence to disprove what she was saying. They just did not want to believe her.

The interviewing officer, DC Moran, took the oath. He was questioned about why Rebecca had been arrested and the interview that had taken place. He accepted during his cross examination that they had no evidence to arrest Rebecca. They had simply found letters and documents at Raj's house with the name Rebecca Turner. They had arrested Rebecca as a fishing expedition with the hope of finding something.

Everything Rebecca had then told them had been used against her...

A good reason to do a no comment interview and not be open and honest, Rebecca thought.

She'd fallen into the same trap she had advised clients about day after day.

Matthew asked DC Moran, about the interview, when he had stated that it was for Rebecca to prove where all her money had come from. He had effectively reversed the burden of proof. DC Moran admitted that he was wrong. He went on to excuse the poor investigation into Rebecca's defence saying he was too busy to help with enquires in the case, including contacting witnesses.

'I had enough of my own case load,' he told the court. DC Moran was given a hard time in the witness box. Rebecca was pleased with how Matthew had cross examined him. She hoped the jury could see how the police had conducted their investigation and how unfair it was.

Next to be called was the evidence of DC Simmons, the financial investigator in the case. His evidence was the foundation of the case against Rebecca. After the evidence of DC Moran the police investigation was in question. But as the officer's name was called it appeared that DC Simmons was not at court. A message came through from the Usher.

'The officer's wife has fallen over and he cannot attend today,' she informed the judge.

'Right, we will call evidence out of sequence then. We do not want to waste time,' the judge directed.

Rebecca was suspicious. She felt that DC Moran had given a 'heads up' to DC Simmons and he simply was not ready to answer questions. He needed another day to revise over his figures and justify his conclusions.

Evidence relating to Raj's assertion that he was clocking cars was called. An expert gave evidence that clocking cars would not accumulate that much profit over the period alleged. Matthew had no questions for the expert. Rebecca had no knowledge of cars being clocked and did not know whether it was true or not. Raj's barrister cross examined the witness. She maintained that that type of profit was unusual from clocking cars. It hadn't been a good day for Raj's camp by the time the court broke.

Rebecca's family had been at court every day. Her aunties and uncles continued to support her. They sat in court in the public gallery and gave reassuring smiles at tense moments. Rebecca realised the stress they must be all under. Not one of them showed it to her. They stayed strong and showed a united front.

Each day was emotionally draining. Every night Rebecca felt mentally exhausted and as the days passed she struggled to keep up the momentum. Every evening was the same... eating what she could manage of dinner, then reading through her case papers.

'There must be something in here to prove my innocence.' She searched for the same thing every night, reading the same documents over and over.

The following day, DC Simmons was at court. 'How's your wife?' she heard the usher ask him. 'My wife?' He looked confused. 'Oh, yes, yes she's fine,' he stammered. Rebecca was sure she was right. He had just been buying time.

DC Simmons was called. He gave his evidence as to the deposits and withdrawals from Rebecca's account. The deposits started in 2001, before she had even met Raj. The evidence given was that Rebecca had sometimes gone to the bank twice in one day and that the statements taken from Peter and Anne's account did not correlate with the deposits into Rebecca's. The officer was saying that because he couldn't see £100 coming out of Peter and Anne's account, then £100 going into Rebecca's within the next day then that could not be the same money.

Rebecca knew that if her parents had given her money, she might not pay it in straight away if she wasn't near a bank. By that time she may have used some of the cash and only end up paying in £80. Regularly on a night out Rebecca would go to the bank twice as she had spent the money she had with her and wanted to carry on into the night. It was evident from the statements that the second withdrawal was after midnight and always from the bank on the high street in town. This was apparently suspicious... Rebecca thought it was more like normal student behaviour.

In cross examination, Simmons' figures were put into question. He had to accept that he had miscalculated on several occasions and the total amounts reached and attributed to Raj were in fact far too high.

There was a deposit of £9900 into Rebecca's account in 2006. This was money to be used for a deposit on Rebecca's property. Rebecca had withdrawn the money from another account and had to pay it in in cash so that it cleared instantly in time for the completion of the property sale. Rebecca remembered withdrawing the money and walking up the high street to pay it in to the second bank. Although it was clear that the money had been withdrawn from one bank and paid into the other within minutes, DC Simpson had 'missed' this fact and had included the £9900 in the total amount alleged to have been money laundered from Raj.

Matthew was slowly breaking down the total amount of £45000 over six years, which was the amount alleged to have been laundered. By the time he had questioned each amount separately, DC Simmons's evidence looked farcical. He had just taken everything that had been paid into Rebecca's account and added it together. He had not considered the origin of the money and had put it all down to money from Raj.

The prosecution evidence of DC Carter was called. She was the officer in the case. She had been there at Rebecca's arrest, her interview and at every hearing thereafter. She had full conduct of the case and it was her job and duty to investigate, impartially, all aspects of it.

Each officer questioned maintained that they could not comment on each other's behaviour during the investigation.

They closed ranks and pleaded ignorance. Carter accepted that she had not contacted any of Rebecca's witnesses despite being given all of their details from the off. She had no good reason for not doing so other than that she was busy with other cases. She accepted that she had not fulfilled her role adequately.

Kallow jumped to his feet to ask the judge to remind the jury that the police failings were not a reason to acquit, and although 'they may have sympathy with Ms Turner, their decision should not be based on it.'

Mr Khan was Raj's accountant. Rebecca had never met him. The piece of paper that Rebecca had jotted things down on for Raj was seized by the police from Mr Khan. It was that piece of paper that formed that whole second count against her... the paper was disguising criminal property.

Mr Khan was called to give his evidence. He confirmed that he was contacted by Raj to complete his tax returns. He was aware of the investigation against his sister, Suri and had had two meetings with Raj and his family as he prepared his accounts. Khan confirmed that he had not been given any receipts by Raj and that his figures were purely based on details given by Raj about sales and purchases he had made. Khan confirmed that he had submitted the relevant tax returns to the revenue. He showed the piece of paper that Rebecca had written on to the court and jury. He stated, on oath, that he had not relied on or used the figures on the paper at all. He had taken no notice of them.

In short, what Khan had confirmed that he had done for Raj was more than Rebecca had done. The only differences between their actions was that Rebecca had had a relationship with Raj previously and that Khan had in fact filled in official forms and submitted them as the truth.

After Khan's evidence, Matthew made legal submissions to the judge in the absence of the jury. He argued that the piece of paper had not been used by Mr Khan and that it had not in fact disguised anything from anybody. The prosecution argued that it did not matter if anything had actually been disguised, or if Rebecca had actually intended to disguise anything. It could have just been jotting on a piece of paper, criminal property had still been disguised, as the money it referred to was from illegal activities and was being described as legitimate funds.

The judge referred to the Proceeds of Crime Act and agreed that the prosecution was right. Legally, it did not matter what Rebecca intended, or what had actually been disguised or if, in fact, it had actually been disguised from anyone. Rebecca shook her head in the dock. How can this be an offence? she thought. Surely, you have to intend to do something wrong to commit a crime? This was obviously no longer the case. Rebecca was losing her faith in the system.

Rebecca and Raj continued to sit side by side whilst trying to portray a distance to the jury. Despite the outward impression of separation, Rebecca was feeling herself growing closer and closer to Raj as each day passed. The feelings that she had once rejected and moved on from were returning. She began to feel strong emotional ties to Raj. She felt safer because he was next to her. He had promised to protect her and not let anything happen to her. She still trusted him.

Rebecca's parents were still outside the courtroom and could not see what was happening between Raj and Rebecca. The rest of her family however could only watch helplessly as they saw the connection reignite.

The prosecution case finished with the interviews of Raj and Rebecca. They were the complete opposite. Raj had said nothing throughout. He had not even been asked about Rebecca and so had been unable to discuss her role with the police. Raj interviews had taken place before much of the evidence had been gathered and therefore he was not questioned about anything of any substance. Rebecca thought... There was such weak evidence against him at interview... I would have advised a no comment interview if he were my client too.

Rebecca's interviews were fishing expeditions. They asked as much detail as possible about Raj, their relationship and her knowledge and involvement with drugs. Rebecca had been completely frank and honest in her first interview. With Duncan, in her second interview, she had submitted a prepared statement giving more limited information but answering questions put forward. To be fair, she had just been handed copies of her bank account deposits for the past seven years and asked to account for each and every one. She couldn't have done that even if she had wanted to.

After the jury were read the interviews, the prosecution case was closed. All their evidence had been heard. It was the defence's turn. It was now Rebecca's chance to tell her side.

CHAPTER NINETEEN

Raj went first. He had been advised not to give evidence. The prosecution case against him was based on circumstantial evidence. The money in Suri's account, his association with others who had been convicted of drug dealing, his fingerprints on the outside of scales with traces of heroin on them and the phone of a known drug user in his possession. No drugs had actually been found, no surveillance was undertaken to prove his involvement, there was nothing concrete against him and he was adamant he was innocent.

His barrister felt that giving evidence could only damage his defence. Rebecca needed Raj to give evidence to tell the jury that she hadn't done anything wrong. He had never had the opportunity to talk about her and support what she had been saying from the outset.

'Do you want me to give evidence?' Raj asked Rebecca. 'I've been advised not to but I'll do it for you if you want me to?'

Rebecca did not want Raj to risk his own defence for her. She knew she was only there because of her association with him but she was still putting him first despite that.

'No, I'll be fine.' She smiled at him. That was probably the first time since she had met him that he had ever offered to put her first. She knew it was his way of trying to make things better. Rebecca still saw the good in him.

Just before Rebecca's defence was due to start, Duncan had a phone call from Suri agreeing to give evidence. Rebecca suspected Raj may have had something to do with her change of heart but she didn't question it. She was just glad that she was helping. Their accounts were almost identical despite not knowing each other before.

'Rebecca Turner.' Matthew turned and looked at Rebecca in the dock. She made her way out through the locked gate and walked up to the witness box. She felt the jury's eyes watching her walk. They were judging her every move. She knew they would judge her every word. It was down to her. It all depended on if these strangers liked her or not.

Rebecca was sworn in. She took the oath on the bible. She was catholic and prayed regularly, even more since the investigation had begun. It was funny how even those with little or no faith turn to God in times of need.

Matthew asked her questions first. He asked open questions about her relationship with Raj. She told the jury exactly what she had told the police. She was completely honest and she hoped that the jury could see that. She felt all eyes in the court focused on her as she described how they had met, their turbulent relationship and how they had eventually split.

Matthew moved on to the financial evidence. Rebecca confirmed three amounts that Raj had given to her and referred the jury to the bills, withdrawal and deposits made in relation to them. All her other deposits related to cash from her parents or cash from friends for social outings. Marie's hen do, Christmas meals and holidays. Rebecca had always been the organiser, booking events and then collecting the cash from others. She would then pay the cash into her account. Why didn't she make notes? Why not keep a record? Because she never thought in a million years that she would be asked questions about it years and years later.

She was asked why she made deposits and then withdrawals on one day. Rebecca explained that her finances had always been disorganised. This was clear from the debt that she had built up from her university days and from renovating her house. She had a hectic social life which meant that last minute plans were common, and trips to the cash point were necessary.

'Twice on the same night?' queried Matthew.

Rebecca explained that she would return to the cash point once she had spent her initial stash. 'Surely this is normal?' Rebecca hoped that the jury could relate to her. There was only one male on the jury that was close to her age, the others were at least ten years older that her... Rebecca just had no way of telling.

Matthew moved on to ask questions about writing on the piece of paper. Rebecca explained that evening like it had happened. She accepted it was her handwriting. She accepted where she had got the figures from but she could not accept that she had purposely tried to hide drug money and help Raj disguise his proceeds of crime.

Rebecca gave her evidence for the whole day. She was exhausted. She knew the hardest part was yet to come. She could not read the jury. A couple of ladies at the front sat next to each other gave very different vibes. One was smiling and nodding along to Rebecca's evidence, while the other scowled and raised her eyebrows in, what Rebecca could only think was disbelief.

The next day Rebecca finished her examination in chief with Matthew. She felt that she had told her story and had the chance to right the wrongs that Kallow had tried to cement in the jury's minds.

It was then Kallow's turn. Kallow started aggressively with a raised stern voice.

'Do you accept that Raj is a drug dealer?'

'No,' Rebecca answered.

'After all the evidence you have heard, you still don't believe it?' He laughed as he listed his own interpretation of the strong case against Raj.

'No, because I was there and it wasn't like you described it. If it was that obvious and it's been going on for years like you say, then why hasn't he been arrested before?'

Kallow ignored Rebecca's question and moved on.

The judge interrupted. 'We are not going to continue like this are we?' he commented. 'Let's calm it down.'

Rebecca was under attack. Kallow wanted her to be convicted, he was desperate for it. Convicting a solicitor would make his career. He would be trusted and respected by the CPS forever more. His case load would be immense. The pound signs gleamed in his eyes.

Hour after hour passed as he asked Rebecca about every single transaction into her account for the past seven years. If she could not be sure exactly where it was from, why not? He suggested that her account movements were suspicious. She answered as best she could. 'Sometimes things do not have a straight answer... it's just the way things are. Things aren't always black and white,' she reasoned. Kallow trawled through deposit after deposit, withdrawal after withdrawal.

A whole day passed with repetitive questions about Rebecca's account and the origins of cash paid into it. By the end of the day Rebecca could not wait to get into bed. She could not keep her eyes open. She had to be on the ball. Each response she gave could be turned and twisted into what Kallow wanted to hear. Every word that left her lips had to be thought about and considered, but her hesitation and pauses were pounced on by Kallow.

Rebecca returned the following day for day three in the witness box. Those accused of murder were not interrogated like she was being. Kallow moved on to Rebecca's relationship with Raj. He suggested over and over that it wasn't as she had described and that she had lived with him for months and months. 'Why else would she have bought him a washing machine?' he told the court.

'As a joint gift for his birthday and a moving in present,' she responded.

'Why would you buy someone that?' The same question was rephrased and asked again and again. Rebecca was growing tired and felt emotional.

'Because I'm kind!' she snapped at Kallow. What did he want her to say? She was telling the truth! Why else do you buy someone a gift? Kallow was suggesting she had been living with Raj as a permanent arrangement. It was frustrating for Rebecca to be told by someone who didn't know her, what had happened in her own life. She knew the truth and she was trying to tell it but was being called a liar.

Kallow discussed Rebecca's arrest. Looking back and remembering it made Rebecca teary. She was tired, emotional and drained. She put her head down and fought back tears as Kallow continued his attack.

'Are you OK?' asked Kallow sarcastically.

'Yes,' Rebecca swallowed. Kallow asked about Rebecca's interview. She tried to answer but tears streamed down her face.

'Are you putting on a little show for the jury? Is that why you're crying?'

'No, I'm crying because I'm upset about what you are saying about me,' Rebecca replied.

'You want the jury to feel sorry for you, don't you? You're putting on an act for them,' Kallow sniped.

'So I'm an actress now as well as everything else I'm supposed to be am I?' Rebecca snapped. She had had enough. She wasn't even allowed to have emotion and be upset about what was happening to her without her being accused of lying and being dishonest.

Kallow continued relentlessly.

'You paid the bills at Raj's house didn't you?'

'No, I didn't. I paid the bills at my house. Where I was living.' Kallow queried payments out of Rebecca's account to gas and electricity providers. 'They are from my property,' she maintained.

Kallow wanted the jury to believe that Rebecca had been settled with Raj at Suri's house and that she had been party to the goings on. Instead of checking their facts about where Rebecca's utility payments had come from the police had just jumped to conclusions and run with it.

After a further day of questions about her bank account and relationship with Raj, Kallow finally changed topic.

Rebecca was asked about the piece of paper that she had written on or DK/1 as it had been formally named in court. Kallow's main focus was that Rebecca must have known about Suri's case when she wrote on the paper and so must have been suspicious that something illegal was going on.

Rebecca's problem was that she did not know exactly when she had found out about Suri's case. She wasn't dating Raj when the investigation had started into his sister and although they had stayed in contact, Raj remained private about his home life and kept his family very separate.

Rebecca would not ask Raj about his family as he was the sort that would get angry and irritated by questions about things which he felt where no one else's business.

In truth Rebecca was not interested in Raj's family life either. She had made a break from him and wanted to move away from that part of her life. She did not want to be worrying about things that really didn't concern her. If Raj wanted to talk about it and wanted her to know, he would tell her. That was the way it had always been between them and things were not going to change now especially after they had split up.

The trial had come three years after Suri had been arrested. Rebecca could not remember the timing of when she knew what and what exactly she was told. It wasn't such an important event to her that she thought she ought to note it down for future reference but this point was one that was laboured by the prosecution. If she knew when she wrote on the paper she must have been suspicious. The truth was she wasn't suspicious and that was all that she could answer. She didn't think she had known at the time but she definitely knew by the time she was arrested. Kallow tried to manipulate the interview as she had spoken openly about her knowledge of Suri's case. It was limited knowledge. It was from what she had seen when she saw Suri's name on the list at court that day.

Sometime after that court hearing, Raj had brought round a restraint order concerning an account in Suri's name. Rebecca explained to Raj what a restraint order was and that it meant that Suri couldn't access or use the money in that account. Rebecca had asked Raj what was going on. He told Rebecca that the money was his money. Suri had put it in her bank account as he did not have one. He explained that because Suri had paid a large amount of money in cash she had to show where it came from. Rebecca knew from work that money was often seized under the proceeds of crime act while enquiries were made. The police could stop you and if you were in possession of over £1000 they could seize it. People would often come into the office enraged at the injustice.

In interview, Rebecca had been asked if she had seen the papers in Suri's case. She replied, 'Yeah, she's shown me them.' She went on to explain she had been shown the restraint order by Raj and not the full prosecution papers known as the committal papers. She stressed seconds later that Raj had shown her them not Suri. Because she had said the word 'she' Kallow suggested over and over that Suri had been round with her papers and that Rebecca had known all about it.

'Why did I say she?' Rebecca questioned. Suri hadn't shown her anything. Seconds later she had clarified the position. Rebecca could only put it down to the stress of the situation in interview. She had no other explanation. Rebecca wished she'd said nothing in interview. She'd been so naïve. That one word could convict her. Kallow was making such a huge deal about it. Emphasizing it to the jury with his facial expression impressing it on them further.

Rebecca had poured her heart out in interview. 'I wasn't looking at him as a suspicious person or someone who was up to no good. I was looking at him as someone that I was with, on and off, for a number of years that I trusted and if he tells me something then I believe that to be true. I had no reason to doubt him.'

She had seen DC Carter and DC Moran exchange looks. They didn't believe a word she said.

Rebecca was never asked in interview when she had found out about Suri's case. She was just asked what she knew then... that was months after writing on the paper DK/1. In that time she had seen Suri in court and Raj had told her some of what was going on. It was again months after that that she had seen the restraint order.

The basis of the prosecution was that Rebecca MUST have been suspicious. They had to establish that she had had a close relationship with Raj and that he had confided in her and gone to her for help. This was far from the reality.

Rebecca stood strong. She was not suspicious. She had no reason to be. If she had been lying she could be more specific about when she found out. She was only vague because she was telling the truth.

Another day passed. A question from the jury was sent up to the judge.

'How could Rebecca's parents afford to give her so much money if her mum is just a teacher?'

Matthew asked for permission to adduce Peter's earnings for 2003. 'For the year in question. £275,000.' Peter told the Court. He had prepared his finances fully as he knew he would be asked about them in detail.

'And how much is your home valued at?'

'2.2 million,' Peter answered.

The jury nodded as if they understood. There was no need for Rebecca to take money from Raj. Her parents supported her and she had her own earnings. Besides that Raj was so tight that he wouldn't have given her a penny even if she asked or begged for it.

Rebecca was relieved her evidence was over. It had been a whole week of being interrogated, called a liar and she felt emotionally drained. She had had a migraine every day and had had to go straight to bed every night through sheer exhaustion.

CHAPTER TWENTY

It was Rebecca's family and friends' turn to support her and give their evidence.

Anne Turner was called first. Rebecca smiled at her mum as she saw her read the oath. She was sad. Seeing her mother having to give evidence was something she never dreamed would happen. She knew her mum would be finding it so difficult. She would be anxious and worried but she never showed it. She seemed so strong. Anne never once showed Rebecca any negative emotion. She stayed positive and reassuring. Rebecca knew that wasn't really how she'd be feeling inside. Anne was going through hell and Rebecca knew it.

Anne and Peter were genuinely two of the nicest people. They were thoughtful, caring and would do anything for anyone.

'They don't deserve this,' Rebecca thought. They weren't the sort of people who had seen the inside of a courtroom, let alone with their daughter in the dock. Rebecca could not believe she had put them through this.

Anne was asked by Kallow about what she knew of Raj.

'I can count the number of times I met him on one hand,' she told the court. 'It wasn't a serious relationship. It wasn't going anywhere,' she added. 'Rebecca was always upset because they were always breaking up then getting back together. It was an immature relationship.'

Anne told the court that Raj had come with Rebecca to a family wedding. Rebecca had missed the family meal before as Raj would not come up a day early for her to attend. He had stayed separate from her family through the whole wedding, sitting in the corner avoiding any conversation. She described seeing Rebecca trying to pull Raj up to dance with her. Raj had pulled away. He didn't want to socialise and made no effort to mix. Anne didn't know Raj at all.

Rebecca had told Anne that Raj bought and sold cars. That was all she knew about Raj's income. Anne told the court what she had been told. She had no need to question her daughter, she accepted what she'd been told. She had no suspicions about Raj.

Anne was asked about money that she had given to Rebecca. 'We supported her as and when needed. We did not document what was given but we gave her cash on a regular basis. We did that with all our children, Rebecca was no different. You can see from our accounts what we could afford. If you ask a particular day what did we give, I could not be precise but I know we gave her thousands over many years.'

Despite Kallow's attempts, he could not discredit Anne. She was an honest witness.

Rebecca was relieved when Anne left the witness box. She knew that would have been so hard for her mum to do. She blinked back tears as she listened to the evidence.

Peter was next. He gave similar evidence to Anne. He told the court of his few meetings with Raj and how he had financially supported his daughter through her studies and initial years of practice. Rebecca watched as her father answered questions. She could see he was nervous. His hands visibly shook as he took the bible and read the oath. It was heartbreaking. She could not believe her family was having to go through this to protect her.

Marie walked up to the witness box and sat straight down. It was her worst nightmare to speak in front of people and Rebecca knew that. Her little sister would never have been a witness through choice. She was doing it to help her.

Marie was asked a similar series of questions. Describe Rebecca's relationship with Raj. What did she know about Raj? What was Rebecca's social role in their friendship group... did she give money to Rebecca for events she had organised?

Marie described the relationship as on and off, she knew little of Raj but had seen more of him than Anne and Peter on a few nights out. She didn't like Raj as she saw Rebecca upset from their continuous break-ups. She blamed Raj for that and felt protective of her sister.

Marie told how Rebecca had organised her hen do and various holidays. Marie herself had had to give money to Rebecca from those she had collected it from for her hen do.

It was strange trying to convince people that the truth was the truth. Each witness told how they had little or no knowledge of Raj because he distanced himself from them. The prosecution manipulated the defence witness's words to blame Rebecca for the distance... 'She was trying to hide him from her friends and family,' they claimed.

Rebecca knew that her witnesses were credible, reliable and genuine. The prosecution could not call them all liars, they were all likeable. Their only option was to twist the truth to make the jury believe that Rebecca had hidden everything from her family and friends.

Rebecca's oldest friend was Jennifer. They had been friends for fifteen years and were as close as sisters. They spent every Saturday night, holiday, heartbreak and celebration together.

Jennifer had been the stand-in every time Raj had not been there. On Anne's 50th birthday, Rebecca had brought Jennifer on the all-expenses paid family holiday. For Peter's 50th birthday, Jennifer had been Rebecca's date. They were invited everywhere as a couple even though Rebecca was in a relationship with Raj. It wasn't that Rebecca didn't ask Raj, he just never wanted to come and would never make the effort for her.

Jennifer stood in the witness box and after taking the oath she looked up and caught Rebecca's eye. Rebecca smiled reassuringly from the dock at the back. It was the first time Jennifer had seen Rebecca there. She began to cry...

'Why are you so upset?' Kallow patronised.

'Because it's upsetting seeing my friend in there when she hasn't done anything wrong,' Jennifer sobbed.

Rebecca hated that this was putting everyone through hell. She didn't want to be the cause of everyone's worry and pain but she couldn't do anything to stop it... it was out of her control.

Just like others, Jennifer confirmed that she had not known much of Raj and what she did know was that he sold cars for a living. She accepted that she had met him on a number of occasions years before and described how he used to upset Rebecca continuously. It was the same old questions from the prosecution and the same answers from the witnesses. They could not be broken.

Nicola, Anita and Annette's evidence followed. Anita broke down in tears and, like Jennifer, explained that it was upsetting seeing what her friend was going through.

Rebecca got the feeling that the jury liked her friends and family. She felt like they believed them. Her only worry was that they would accept the prosecution's assertion that she had hidden things from her friends and family so they did not know the whole truth.

As each believable witness gave their evidence the prosecution became more and more desperate in their questioning. Nicola was asked if she knew what Raj did. She said she didn't. It wasn't something that she had discussed with Rebecca. She was asked if she knew how Raj had paid for things.

'Did you ask how he paid for dinner?'

Nicola replied, 'No,' and she frowned in confusion.

What a ridiculous question, thought Rebecca. Who in their right minds asked how people paid for things? If it wasn't such a serious situation Rebecca would have found it all laughable.

'Did she tell you he dealt in cash?' came the next question...

'No,' Nicola responded still frowning at the ludicrousness of it all.

Rebecca thought about it... she knew what her brother-in-law and Annette's boyfriend did for a job but she genuinely hadn't asked Nicola, Anita or Jennifer what their boyfriends did. It wasn't something that came up in conversation unless it was relevant. She thought about her work colleagues. She didn't know what their other halves did either. Is that abnormal? she thought. She hoped not. The last thing she needed was for the jury to think she was strange. Strange can equal not likeable and suspicious.

After all the live evidence had finished, Matthew read out several character references from partners of local solicitors who had worked alongside Rebecca and had seen, first hand, the type of person she was. Their references were positive. They showed that she was well thought of and supported.

As the defence evidence ended, the closing speeches began.

Kallow stood up and amended the depositing money charge to consist only of the three occasions that Rebecca had herself accepted that the money had come from Raj.

Firstly, from the phone bill that Rebecca had accumulated whilst on holiday in Turkey for two weeks. She had gone with Marie and Jennifer. She had called Raj every day and spoke for hours on her mobile. Raj had promised to split the bill when she got home. The bill came through at £1400. Rebecca couldn't believe it... true to his word Raj gave her £800 towards it. Rebecca had paid it into her account to cover the bill. Her account showed the bill coming out just days later.

Secondly, Raj did not have a bank account and had asked Rebecca to pay his car trader's insurance policy over the phone and he would pay her the money. Rebecca paid the £1100 and took the cash from Raj which she deposited to cover the cost.

Finally, Rebecca had sold Raj her old car when she decided to buy another one. She had a five-year-old Golf Convertible. Raj had paid her the market value. He believed, as a car salesman, that he could make a profit on it. Rebecca paid in £10000 for the car, which she had then used to buy a new one.

Those three deposits had been explained to the police in interview and gone over again in evidence. Rebecca could prove the phone bill, insurance payment and the car purchase. She had been given money by Raj from his business.

Kallow acted like he was doing Rebecca a very huge favour when in reality after the demolition of DC Simmons' evidence, the prosecution knew they had no option but to.

The sum was now laundering cash to the total of £12,500. This was the exact total that Rebecca had accepted as being from Raj from the start. £32,500 had been knocked off just like that. This could have been sorted out before the trial if the officers had investigated and contacted Rebecca's witnesses as requested. Of course when the newspapers said £45,000 in cash had been paid into Rebecca's account it didn't look good. What they didn't tell people was that was over a seven year period and not all of it was cash. Taking off Raj's money that meant that £5500 cash per year had gone into Rebecca's account. That's £450 per month. Anne and Peter used to practically give her that to get to University and Law School on the train. When it was broken down and explained it seemed reasonable and logical.

The prosecution were not willing to drop the count totally despite the fact they had been proved wrong. They still wanted a conviction at all costs.

The speeches started with the prosecution. They started hard dealing with Raj and the allegations of drug dealing.

They asked the jury to find that there was no possible way to account for the money in Suri's account unless it was from ill-gotten gains. They claimed that it must be from drugs due to his association with convicted drug dealers and the phone found at his house which belonged to known drug users. It was all about association. No drugs had been found and no witness had sworn that they had seen him selling anything. It was all circumstantial evidence. None of it was direct. Rebecca still did not accept that he had done what was alleged. She had sat through all the evidence and she knew how things were manipulated to support the prosecution.

The prosecution closing turned to Rebecca... The original first charge had been amended. They now asserted that she had converting criminal property in relation to the three amounts which Rebecca herself had told them had come from Raj. They had dropped the £45,000 as originally claimed. The jury had to decide if Rebecca had been suspicious that Raj's money was from ill gotten gains. She did not have to suspect that it came from drugs just that it came from something illegal. The prosecution had changed the goal posts throughout the trial. As each of their points were hacked down by the defence they amended their targets.

Rebecca's culpability had decreased over the past few weeks. She had gone from the mastermind behind Raj's enterprise, helping him to get out of every scrape and to evade the police to someone who suspected that Raj may have been up to something. She then, without intention, wrote on a piece of paper which was never used and had no effect whatsoever.

When Rebecca thought about it like that she could not believe where she was.

Kallow still wanted her convicted though; he wasn't going to stop whether it was right or wrong.

The defence closing was kicked off by Raj's barrister, Mr Martin. He gave a logical and believable speech which accounted for all of the prosecution evidence and gave a valid explanation for each. Of course Raj had scales at his house with traces of heroin and cocaine on them... Raj's brother was a heroin addict and admitted that they were his scales. The phones at Raj's house had been bought by him from a drug addict desperate to sell them, the texts on the phone where from the addict to his girlfriend and had no connection to Raj. The money in Suri's account was from clocking cars. Raj accepted that this was illegal and pleaded guilty to money laundering before the trial started.

At the end of the closing Rebecca felt positive. Mr Martin had made complete sense. During a break outside the courtroom Rebecca's family were all on a high.

'Excellent speech,' her uncle commented.

Everyone believed for the first time that Raj would get a not guilty verdict. That would certainly mean a not guilty verdict for Rebecca. It would be perverse to find her guilty if they did not find that Raj had done anything wrong.

On returning to court, Matthew began his speech. There was so much to cover with the financial aspects that he could not be as punchy and direct as Mr Martin. Rebecca hoped that the jury would not be buried under the finances and miss the important contradictions in the prosecution evidence. He reiterated what Rebecca had told the jury in her evidence. It was all about Rebecca's suspicions, or lack of them. Ultimately, it was down to whether the jury believed her or not. Rebecca hadn't been able to read the jury.

Before the jury went out the judge had to sum up the case and direct the jury as to the law surrounding the charges. Rebecca was anxious that the jury would not understand properly. It was a new and complex area of law which took trained professionals time to get their heads around... she wondered if the jury could really grasp it .

The judge began with the evidence on Raj. He directed the jury exactly as the bench book sets out but the tone of his voice made it very clear what his feelings were on the matter.

'IF you believe the defendant,' his cynical tone boomed out across the court.

Rebecca's mood flattened. The good work of Mr Martin was demolished with a single sentence. Rebecca knew Raj was going to be convinced. Raj knew it too. The judge spoke with such venom that his opinion was apparent to the entire court. Although a biased summing up could be grounds for appeal, the judge gave a summing up which was completely by the book on paper. It was his tone and accompanying expressions that had done the damage.

As the judge moved on to his summing up about Rebecca his tone softened. He set out the evidence for both the prosecution and the defence evenly. He stressed Rebecca's good character and supporting evidence from friends and family. He drew to the jury's attention that Rebecca was well thought of and notably good at her job. He directed the jury to have no sympathy for Rebecca in relation to the poor investigation by the police. He told them that although this was incorrect the jury should not consider that when looking at whether or not she was guilty.

The jury was sent out and Rebecca looked up as they walked past her. Few looked up and locked eyes, a couple of those smiled reassuringly. Rebecca was worried by the ones that lowered their heads to avoid eye contact. Her life was now in their hands.

CHAPTER TWENTY-ONE

Each minute felt like hours. Rebecca and her family waited outside the courtroom for the jury to return. Every time the tannoy called other cases Rebecca's heart jumped into her mouth.

Her fear that it would be her name they called made her heart beat so fast it felt like she would pass out.

She made a joke of it to her friends and family. She knew they were feeling the same and she felt guilty that they were having to go through this. She could see the frightened look in their faces when the announcements began. It was harder for them in a way. Whatever the outcome she knew she would have to deal with it. She knew she would cope. She had no choice but to. She told herself that there would be life after this, no matter what the outcome was. Her family, especially Anne, Peter and Marie, would struggle. Rebecca knew this. They would feel helpless and would be unable to manage the worry if she were to be sent to prison. This was not their life. This was not what they should have to deal with. She had unknowingly dragged them into a completely different world.

As the minutes slowly ticked by the end of the day still seemed forever away. For over a year Rebecca had been waiting for this to end but now she was here she was scared of what it might bring. Everyone tried to fill their time with chit chat whilst the ominous decision loomed. They were all feeling it.

Matthew approached Rebecca as she sat with her mum and dad.

'We are being called back in,' he told them. 'We don't know what for.' They looked nervously at each other. Rebecca took a deep breath and smiled reassuringly at both her parents as the tannoy called her case.

As they settled in court, Raj looked at Rebecca.

'Do you know why we've been called in?' he asked her.

'No,' she said anxiously. 'I don't think anyone does.'

'You'll be OK,' Raj nodded, sensing the nerves in Rebecca's voice, 'nothing's going to happen to you.'

He seemed so sure that Rebecca felt instantly more at ease. 'That's right,' she told herself, 'nothing can happen to you. You haven't actually done anything.'

Deep down Rebecca didn't know though. She genuinely couldn't call this one. With cases that she had run herself she had been able to predict the likely outcome and had, on most occasions, been right but with her own case she couldn't read it. She knew that the jury could be buying the prosecution's fairytale.

'Court rise.'

The judge entered as everyone stood.

'I'm going to send the jury home for the night,' he told the court. 'They do not seem close to coming to a verdict and it's been a long day. Deliberations can continue with fresh heads tomorrow.'

Rebecca didn't know whether she was relieved or horrified. Part of her wanted it over but part of her was terrified of what was to come. Yet another night of worry and no sleep for her entire family.

The jury were called in by the judge and discharged for the evening. They were told to return bright and early the next day. As the jury were led out again, Rebecca tried to read them. She just wanted a little sign that everything was going to be fine, or that just one of them believed her. She got nothing.

As Raj was taken downstairs to the cells, he turned to Rebecca and smiled. She could tell he was just as scared as she was but was trying to be supportive and positive for her. She could read his eyes though. He was frightened and that frightened her just as much.

After about an hour of broken sleep Rebecca returned to court the following day with her family and closest friends. Each one looked as exhausted as the next. She could see they were all struggling. Each had the same painted positive face with the same anguish underneath.

Everyone was called back into court as the jury was formally sent out to recommence their discussions.

The waiting outside the courtroom then continued. It was by far the most painful part of the proceedings. The torturous waiting seemed to be endless.

Hour after hour passed. The tannoy continued to blurt out directions for the next court hearings which made Rebecca's heart skip a beat each time.

Lunch time came. Most people couldn't bear to eat. Rebecca on the other hand had gone completely the opposite way and ate constantly. This was not good either as the comfort eating only made her feel sick and unwell.

The afternoon dragged on and on until finally Matthew approached as she sat with her aunties.

'There's a verdict on three of the counts,' he informed them. 'We don't know which three counts or who they relate to but the jury are coming back in. It could be a mixture of the both of you.'

Rebecca felt instantly panicked. Three counts meant it was likely that they had decided on Raj first. He had three counts and Rebecca had two. Raj had two counts of supplying class A drugs and one count of money laundering connected to his brother's fake receipt.

Rebecca's emotions overcame her and for the first time in front of her family and friends she broke down in tears. Her aunties gathered round her as Anne rushed from the other side of the waiting room to hold her in her arms. Rebecca sobbed uncontrollably. It was a year of emotions pouring out. As she tried to compose herself, Rebecca looked around and saw each and every one of her friends and family wiping their eyes. They had all been brought to tears at the sight of her distress. Rebecca saw an officer that she had dealt with regularly on a professional basis standing by a courtroom door. He had seen what had just happened and he shook his head in disgust at the situation. Rebecca could see that there were people on her side.

Anne sat Rebecca down while her aunties scrambled around in their bags to find tissues and make-up to clean up her tear stained face. As they dabbed her tears away Anne spoke quietly to Rebecca.

'Rebecca listen to me seriously, you cannot react if they come back with guilty verdicts for Raj. The jury will be looking for it. The prosecution want to see a connection between you two. That's what they are looking for. Look at me,' she said sternly. 'Do you understand? You cannot react. You must keep looking straight forward. You hold back those tears. If the jury see them they will think what the prosecution has been saying is true.'

Rebecca nodded. She understood. It was going to be so difficult for her. She did care for Raj and she did care what happened to him. If anything, this case had just pushed them even closer together.

They all marched into the courtroom and Raj was already there. He knew that they had a verdict on three... he knew it was him. They didn't really speak to each other. Neither knew what to say but both were feeling exactly the same.

The jury entered. Their body language gave nothing away.

'Have you reached a verdict on all counts on which you have all agreed?' asked the clerk.

'No,' replied the forewoman of the jury.

She was a stern looking black woman who looked like she took no nonsense. Rebecca hadn't had a good vibe from her since the trial had started. She had always had a disapproving look throughout the evidence. Rebecca knew the worst was about to come as soon as she stood up as forewoman.

Rebecca looked over to Cassidy, the second prosecution barrister. She could see he was on his laptop playing a word game.

So nice to know he is taking this so seriously, Rebecca thought. Just another job to him. He doesn't even give the effects a second thought.

'Have you reached a unanimous verdict on any of the counts?' continued the clerk.

'Yes, Counts 1 to 3.'

Rebecca looked straight forward and didn't react. They weren't her counts. They were all to do with Raj. If they thought Raj was not guilty it followed that she couldn't be guilty either. Rebecca held her breath.

'On count one... That Raj Singh was concerned in the supply of heroin, how do you find?'

'Guilty,' the forewoman answered. It hit Rebecca like a tonne of bricks but she could not react. She wanted to look at Raj and comfort him but she had to be an emotionless robot.

The second count of being concerned in the supply of cocaine was read. It followed that they would find Raj guilty of both.

'Guilty,' the forewoman replied.

'Count three... conspiring with Gilly Singh to disguise criminal property by drafting fraudulent receipts relating to being a car trader.... how do you find?'

'Not guilty.' The forewoman answered with not a shred of emotion in her voice.

Rebecca often thought that juries should be given a rough estimate of the implications of their verdict before their deliberations. Many experts and critics felt that this would affect the jury decision making process as although sometimes in law someone may be guilty the jury may feel that they do not deserve the sentence that would follow.

Rebecca thought that their decision regarding Raj would not be altered regardless. It was clear the jury didn't like him and he hadn't endeared himself to them by not giving evidence and explaining himself.

Legally Rebecca felt that the evidence wasn't there and there was not enough to convict him on. How anyone could be SURE that he had been concerned in the supply of class A drugs based on the prosecution case was unbelievable. He didn't really have to give evidence and answer the accusations but a jury sees that exercising that right is suspicious. They like people to explain themselves... Rebecca had done that from the start but it hadn't helped her so far.

GUILTY... the word rang in Rebecca's head. She continued to look forward, still standing as the jury were led out and discharged for the day. They were to return the next day to start dissecting the case against her. She couldn't look over at Raj as she knew it would break her.

As soon as the last jury member walked out she sat straight down. She put her head down and cried. Tears streamed down her face. She knew what this meant. He was looking at double figures in custody. He was 35 already. He wouldn't be released until he was well into his 40s. His chance to have children and settle down had just been cut down to next to nothing. Rebecca cried for him.

As she put her head down she felt an arm around her. It was Raj. Usually embarrassed by any form of affection, Raj was trying to comfort Rebecca and reassure her. He should have been distraught but his attention was on Rebecca. The judge was still talking in the background but it just sounded like a dubbed noise. She didn't know what was being said.

Then three words seemed to come out of nowhere... 'Take him down.'

The guard stood up and pulled Raj by the arm towards the cell door. This would be the last time Rebecca would see him... possibly ever. She turned and peered at him through her tears, still gulping to steady her breath. Raj looked at her and smiled... 'I love you,' he told her. She didn't even have the chance to reply as he was hurried through the door which was slammed instantly behind him. Rebecca just stood there in shock. What had just happened?

She looked over to the public gallery where all her friends and family were waiting for her. They were shocked by the verdict but not saddened by it. They didn't believe what the prosecution had said as they knew the lies that they had told about Rebecca but there was no love lost between Raj and Rebecca's close ones. They had seen him destroy her emotionally during their relationship and now had seen him destroy her professionally during the trial.

Outside court Duncan waited with Matthew. 'Go home and get some rest ready for tomorrow,' he advised. 'We just don't know what that jury are thinking. Be prepared for anything.'

The journey home had become all so familiar. Anne heard people whispering as they walked past them towards the car park.

'That's that solicitor,' one woman told another. It had become the norm and Rebecca wasn't fazed by it. She just let it go over her head. People who didn't know her didn't matter... and those that did were behind her.

After another sleepless night, Rebecca prepared for her D-Day. As the court was called in it was strange being in the dock on her own. She was used to Raj being in there with her. It had been a comfort to be sharing the experience with someone. He had been a silent support. Rebecca felt lonely and vulnerable in the dock despite seeing her family and friends with reassuring smiles from the public gallery. The guards had become attached to Rebecca and the case. They all believed that she would be acquitted. Some of them knew her from working in the courts before the investigation had begun. Even though Lynne, the female guard, was there to supervise Rebecca she actually felt that she was on her side and in a strange way it made her feel safer.

As the jury was sent out, Rebecca's waiting continued. Matthew and Duncan called her into a conference room to talk.

'Like we said to you last night you must be prepared for anything. If you are convicted you could be remanded into custody awaiting sentence.'

'Do I need to pack a bag?' Rebecca asked, wide-eyed.

She couldn't actually believe she'd been so naive. Of course she should have brought a bag. She should have been prepared to go to prison. She had had to tell people the same thing herself so many times... why had she been so stupid?

'Yes you do.' Matthew and Duncan nodded to each other.

'OK,' Rebecca said cheerily, putting on a front. She had to take a deep breath while she went and told her family about the conversation. She couldn't go and get anything herself as she wasn't allowed out of the building. She knew that what she was about to say would frighten everyone.

'I have to go and get a toothbrush, toiletries and underwear just in case.'

'Just in case what?' Anne gasped in horror. 'What do you mean?'

Rebecca could hear the panic in Anne's voice.

130

'It's in case they come back with a guilty verdict and I get remanded until they sentence me.'

Rebecca tried to be as blasé about it as possible. She wasn't scared about prison. It wasn't the unknown to her because of her job but she was scared of what it would do to her family.

Rebecca wasn't allowed out of the court building while the jury were out. She had to wait in case they were called in. Rebecca's auntie and uncle offered to go into the town and get her all the necessities she might need.

'It's OK, Anne, we will go and sort it all out. Leave it to us,' offered Uncle Gareth.

The jury could have come back at any time. They might not even make it back in time to give Rebecca the things they'd bought. Once she was in custody she couldn't be handed anything in the cells. All she could take was whatever was in the dock with her.

Thirty minutes later Gareth and his wife Cate, ran up the steps of the court hot and out of breath. They had clearly rushed around getting everything they could think of. They had bought her a bag and packed it. Rebecca was so grateful.

'Thank you,' she told them genuinely. Her family had been her rock during the case. They had been so supportive in every way possible. Rebecca was overwhelmed by their generosity.

The wait continued. As Rebecca waited in the court lobby she saw others being called into different courts. Some emerged ecstatic, so relieved that it was all over. Others did not come out of the court door again. Their families left heartbroken and inconsolable. Rebecca wondered which one she would be.

Rebecca was summoned into the courtroom. The jury entered.

'Have you reached a verdict on which you all agree?'

'No,' the forewoman told the court. 'We cannot agree.'

Rebecca didn't know how she felt about that. Some people must have thought she was a liar. They must have believed what had been said about her.

The judge went on to give a majority direction. He told the jury that if 10 or 11 of them could agree then they would accept that as a verdict. It had been a long day already so the judge sent the jury home to return in the morning.

'Some people in there are fighting for you,' Auntie Denise told Rebecca. They aren't going to give up on you. They won't let you down.'

Rebecca hadn't thought about it like that before but Denise was right. For every someone who doubted her there was someone on her side.

Anne and Peter took Rebecca shopping to get all the extras she needed for her prison bag. Gareth and Cate had done a brilliant job but there were still a couple of things she needed to add to the bag.

It was surreal. Buying paper, envelopes, stamps, books, toiletries and clothes. They bought a bigger holdall and packed it full. Anne later told Rebecca that it was one of the most distressing times of her life, shopping for her daughter's prison property.

'It'll stay with me for the rest of my life,' she said sadly.

The next morning, Rebecca arrived at court with her bag packed and her army of faithful supporters by her side. The jury were sent out to continue their deliberations.

Hours passed and nothing. The barristers began talking about it being a hung jury. This was when the jury could not reach a unanimous or a majority decision. It meant that there was no verdict and the prosecution would have to decide whether there would be a retrial at a later date.

'She'll be convicted next time,' Kallow cackled. 'We will take her to trial again. We can put in Raj's conviction as being concerned in the supply of drugs next time and that'll go against her. We will get her.'

Rebecca didn't know why she was so shocked at how callous he was. He had been like it throughout the trial. He revelled in the misery of Rebecca, her family and her friends.

Rebecca's family listened carefully as Matthew explained that there was a possibility of a retrial if the jury could not reach a verdict.

'My God, we will have to go through this all over again?' Cate exclaimed. It was what everyone was thinking. They were all at their limits and did not know how much more they could take.

The judge resumed the court. He asked the jury for a final time if they had reached any verdict on either count.

'We haven't.' The forewoman shook her head.

'Is it likely that you could agree if you were given any extra time?'

The jury exchanged glances. 'No,' the woman replied. 'We cannot agree.'

The judge sighed. Kallow sprung to his feet.

'I have taken advice from those instructing me and I can confirm that we will be seeking a retrial.'

The blonde female that had turned her nose up and shook her head during Rebecca's evidence yelled 'Yes!' with glee. It was clear what her vote had been. She was obviously sure Rebecca was guilty.

'Sure,' Rebecca snorted, 'what a joke. How can someone be SURE that I have done something that I haven't done? The whole thing is a farce.'

Duncan was stunned.

'I have never in all my years of practice seen a reaction from a jury member like that. That was unbelievable,' he told Rebecca.

The judge was anxious that a new trial date be fixed for as soon as possible. He clearly did not want to draw it out for any longer than absolutely necessary. A date was fixed for five months later. Rebecca felt like the nightmare was never going to end.

CHAPTER TWENTY-TWO

Rebecca was stuck in the office at work. Her suspension from going to court, the police station and on prison visits was still in force. She was determined to carry on at work. She didn't want the case to consume her.

Everyone had started to find out about Rebecca's case. She had continued to be in the paper week in week out. She was being recognised by clients. It amused Rebecca that this in fact had a positive effect. The clients seemed to enjoy that Rebecca had personally been caught up in a criminal case. It was like she was one of them. They felt that she could empathise with them so they trusted her more. Rebecca did not try to hide what was going on. She wouldn't bring it up with everyone directly but she wouldn't be embarrassed about it. If she was asked she would talk openly about it.

She was making a mental note of all the people that had snubbed her or made nasty cruel comments. She would remember those that had been there and those that hadn't.

Anne and Peter continued to subsidise Rebecca for the money she was losing for not being able to go to the police station for overtime. They were around a lot more than they used to be. They seemed to base themselves near Rebecca and only go up to their main house for sporadic visits. Rebecca was grateful. She needed them around.

Rebecca felt surprisingly emotionally calm. Physically signs of stress were beginning to show. Rebecca had been suffering with a rash all over her neck which she first thought was an allergic reaction due to its severity. When the rash didn't fade after weeks and weeks Rebecca realised what had caused it. Rebecca hadn't had a period since the trial had begun. It was her body shutting down from the stress she was under. Rebecca preferred to have the physical reaction that she was having. The alternative was a mental overload like a nervous breakdown. She wasn't going to let that happen. She felt that that was what they wanted to happen. They wanted to break her but she wasn't going to let them win. No matter what happened she was determined to come out of this the other side smiling.

The next trial would be all about Rebecca. She would be on her own in the dock. Matthew was essentially on his own. He had no one to help organise the paperwork or to make detailed notes. The prosecution had Kallow and Cassidy as well as a clerk sitting behind them to assist when needed. Duncan applied to the court for a second barrister for Rebecca. She hoped it would even things out more and give Matthew the chance to stay on top of the court paperwork when things were moving at such a fast pace during the trial.

The application was refused. The judge did not feel that a second barrister was needed. The defence were always on the back foot. Rebecca felt that it was unfair. The prosecution had the resources. They had the police to investigate for them while the defence did not have the ability to gather the same standard of information. The defence were always playing catch up. Once again Rebecca told herself not to be surprised. She knew this was the way it was. She had had to deal with it on a daily basis in her professional life.

Rebecca thought back to her regular visits to the police station. She missed being involved in that side of things. She remembered many heated arguments with officers during interviews. A lot of officers were aggressive. They didn't like solicitors.

Rebecca remembered a case when a lady had found out her husband of ten years and father of their three children had cheated on her. She had walked in on him in the pub with another woman. She went over, poured his drink over his head and slapped him round the back of the head. A reasonable reaction most people might think but technically and legally an assault. The officer dealing with the case treated the distressed lady like she had committed a murder. She was someone who had not been arrested before and was highly unlikely to be again. The officer had no empathy whatsoever with the situation which she found herself in. Rebecca pointed out that a caution would be appropriate disposal in the circumstances and that it wasn't in the public interest to proceed with matters any further.

It was decided that a prepared statement would be submitted in interview which would admit the assault, which was a necessary admission for a caution. This angered the officer. Rebecca interjected as the officer asked inappropriate questions. The officer had told Rebecca, 'I can ask anything I want in this interview. It's my interview and I can say what I want.'

Rebecca reminded the officer that there were rules and regulations that he had to follow and that he was not able to ask any questions he liked. They had to be relevant at least! She further reminded the officer that his role was to investigate impartially, not to give opinion and make personal comments. Officers often forgot that that was in fact their actual role.

Television programmes and films have allowed the public to form the inaccurate opinion that officers are there to solve a case and shout at the suspect until they crack in interview.

Unfortunately, officers seem to be under the same misconception. Cases like this were all too familiar to Rebecca. But she did miss trying to make a difference and protect people from poorly trained and aggressive officers.

CHAPTER TWENTY-THREE

As the second trial approached, Rebecca checked the post and fax machine obsessively to see if any new evidence had been sent through about her case. Even if she felt unwell she never had a day off work in case that was the day that something came in.

The prosecution had indicated at court that they wanted to serve new evidence from a handwriting expert. They had suggested during the trial that Suri's indictment had Rebecca's handwriting on it. They had no evidence to back this up. It was simply not true either. Rebecca hadn't even seen the indictment, let alone written on it.

The prosecution were trying to suggest to the jury that Rebecca had been involved with Raj during Suri's case and that she had tried to help them to craft a defence. Suri had her own solicitors and Rebecca had not been in a relationship with Raj at the time.

Kallow had raised the handwriting issue and tried to plant the seed with the jury. They had been told to disregard it but the damage had already been done. The jury would be in their room after trial trying to compare Rebecca's handwriting as if they were the experts and she knew that they would come to their own conclusion regardless of what the judge told them to do.

Rebecca wanted the prosecution to get a handwriting expert. It was not her writing. At least once they had an expert to tell them that they could stop throwing low balls. Suri had even admitted in her evidence that it was her handwriting but Kallow tried to counterbalance this by asking her, 'Has anyone told you to say that?'

Duncan had instructed their own handwriting expert. The report came through. It confirmed exactly what Rebecca had said all along. It wasn't her handwriting. The expert had also in fact compared the writing on DK/1 and said there was no certainty that that was Rebecca's handwriting either. That, of course, actually was Rebecca's. She had admitted it in interview. Why shouldn't she? Rebecca regretted how honest she had been in that first interview. She should have just said nothing and they would have struggled to prove she'd written anything. Rebecca learned a valuable lesson, honesty is not always the best policy. Not that she should have lied but that she should have said nothing at all. The police hadn't listened to her anyway except for the parts that helped them. Those bits had to be the truth of course but the rest was all lies.

A new indictment came through the fax machine one day. It had one count only on it. The disguising criminal property charge relating to DK/1 and the 'false accounts' Rebecca had supposedly made. The indictment was accompanied by an opening in which the prosecution had completely changed tact.

Rebecca spoke to Duncan.

'Have they dropped one of the counts?' she asked.

Duncan phoned the CPS lawyer in charge.

'Yes,' he told Rebecca, 'they are proceeding with just the one count.'

Rebecca was at first ecstatic. It made things seem less serious. They finally accepted that she hadn't taken money from Raj and washed it through her bank account.

Rebecca's mood then darkened. This is too good to be true. They were going all guns blazing before and now to back down. There had to be more to it.

Duncan called a conference with Matthew.

'By dropping that count they are stopping the officers having to give evidence. The jury will not be aware of how they failed to investigate properly, they won't hear the officers giving evidence to such a poor standard. They were not likeable witnesses. They gave the first jury an insight into why you had been brought to court.'

It was now clear that the other count had helped Rebecca's case. The first jury had sympathy because of the witch hunt which she had to endure; that would all be lost without the first count. That was why the prosecution had dropped it. It was a tactical decision. The prosecution could get rid of all the negative sides of their case and still try to get a conviction.

They could also now put in Raj's conviction plus his previous convictions which the original jury had not been aware of. Rebecca was aware of them. They were for violence, mainly drunken fights outside pubs when alcohol had been involved. Raj could not stand being made to feel like or look like an idiot so if he felt like someone was doing that he would lash out. That was his character. Rebecca had never been there when that had happened and she had always accepted his reasoning as to why it had happened. This was a big negative point to be in front of the jury though and Rebecca knew it.

Raj and his family had been sentenced after the first trial. Rebecca didn't attend but Duncan sent along a clerk to make notes at the back of the court. Rebecca wanted to be there but could not show that she was bothered by it.

She knew that Raj would be looking at double figures. She was not sure if his family would be sent to prison with him.

Rebecca waited back at the office for the clerk to return. She was watching the clock. That familiar anxiety passed over her.

'15 years,' she heard the clerk telling Duncan as he strutted in. Rebecca felt sick.

'My God.' That was worse than she had expected. That would be seven and a half years of his life gone. She knew Raj would be shocked by it too. It was a long long sentence. Rebecca suspected that the judge blamed Raj for dragging everyone into it. He had passed a sentence that, realistically, could not be appealed but that was certainly at the top end of the guidelines.

Rebecca felt like crying for Raj. She knew she should think he deserved it, that's what everyone else would think, but she could not bring herself to.

Raj called Rebecca that night. She was relieved to hear from him. He was surprisingly upbeat. 'My brief says it's excessive so we will definitely be able to appeal it and get it squashed.' Rebecca didn't have the heart to tell him it was quashed. He seemed so positive, Rebecca was relieved.

There had been so much press at the time of the first trial, especially in the local press. Most people would have been aware of the ongoing case. The jury pond is a group of people from the local area who would have been exposed to the reports in the weekly paper, including front page photographs of Rebecca. It was only a few months before and not easily forgotten. The next jury would remember it Rebecca was sure of that.

The first count was focused on mainly in the articles. They had quoted the prosecution as saying that Rebecca had paid '£45,000 into her account'. That was the shock factor. It was what people remembered. Nothing was printed about the case being a hung jury or that the amount had been reduced as the prosecution had accepted that Anne and Peter had shown where the money had come from.

All the new jury had to do was have a vague recollection of the case and Google it. Yes, they would be advised by the judge that they should not do that but no one would be shocked to know that the majority of jury members do their own private research. The fact that they would be aware but would see no outcome would leave questions in their head that could prejudice the case.

Duncan and Matthew planned to apply for the case to be moved out of the area to a court where jury members would have seen limited coverage and were less likely to remember it. It was a difficult application. The judge would want to keep the case. After the summing up in the last trial Rebecca wanted him to keep the case too. She had given evidence in front of him for days, he had seen the support she had, she felt he was the best person to oversee it. It was just in the wrong area.

Rebecca did not feel that she could have a fair trial now that the first count had been dropped. The prosecution had left their decision until so close to the new trial that the application to move the trial would have to be made on the first day. This made things even more difficult as the trial would have to be delayed further and considering how long things had been going on already the judge would be very reluctant to agree.

An analysis of texts from Raj's phone had been served on the defence. There wasn't anything that caused Rebecca any trouble. It just showed that they were in contact when they had split up. Rebecca had never denied this. They had always been in contact but just not as regularly.

Importantly there was one text from Raj saying that he was sorry for the way he had treated Rebecca and that he had lost her because of it. If anything this supported Rebecca's case. She had always said that Raj had been selfish and unkind at times in their relationship and that in the end it had just chipped away and destroyed it. The prosecution had always tried to say that this was Rebecca trying to distance herself from him.

At least the text backs me up, Rebecca thought.

She was still worried about the retrial as she didn't know how the change in prosecution tactics could affect things. The jury would only have half the picture. The last jury had got it wrong about Raj. They had bought the prosecution's story. A story was exactly what it was. It made Rebecca think about all the times she had read things in the paper and watched things on the TV about real life crime. They were how the prosecution and the police had pieced things together following their own theory.

How many of these theories were actually right? Rebecca thought. From her experience she doubted many of them.

During the conference with Matthew, Rebecca felt like she was being interrogated. Rebecca had had to ask questions herself in the past with clients but she knew how they felt now. Every question she answered she felt like no one believed her answer. She was going red and became really conscious of her body language. She felt like everyone was analysing her answers and thinking the worst.

Rebecca couldn't let it all get on top of her, she was becoming more negative. She didn't feel like this at the first trial but things were different this time. She knew it would be harder to fight. Some of the last jury hadn't believed her and what if the next jury didn't?

Rebecca's family tried to keep her positive.

'We only need another hung jury,' they told her.

Rebecca knew that the prosecution would go for her again if that happened. They could go to retrial as many times as they wanted but usually they went no more than three. Rebecca knew that would be her. They wouldn't want to drop it until they had no option but to. They would be too scared about Rebecca going after them for malicious prosecution.

Duncan told Rebecca that she had to prepare her witnesses. She had to put each of her friends on standby and tell them that they may have to go through giving evidence again. Rebecca didn't want everyone to have to go through it again and although they wouldn't enjoy the experience she knew that each of them would do it again for her. She knew she had the best friends in the world. The case had cleared all the hangers on and helped Rebecca to get rid of those who weren't true friends.

Duncan had tried to get hold of Suri. She was the most important witness for Rebecca. She could confirm that Rebecca had not had anything to do with helping her prepare for her case and that she herself did not accept Raj's conviction. If Raj's own sister who he lived with did not see any evidence of drug dealing, how could Rebecca be expected to know?

Rebecca believed Suri. She was an honest witness. She had agreed at the end of the last trial that she would give evidence again for Rebecca. Rebecca needed her but on the other hand Rebecca thought it was the least she could do after her brother had dragged Rebecca and her family to hell and back.

Duncan had trouble getting hold of Suri. She was avoiding his call. Rebecca understood her reluctance. She had been traumatised by the case. She had been through years of stress and worry that had clearly taken its toll on her both mentally and physically. She looked ill. Rebecca hadn't remembered her being like that before.

Rebecca just hoped Suri would do the right thing. Rebecca was in exactly the same place that she had been in before she walked free. Suri could help and she should help no matter how difficult it was for her.

When Duncan finally spoke to Suri he tried to address her concerns. She just did not want to step foot in a court again. She wanted to put the past behind her and not look back.

'I just don't know if we can rely on her,' Duncan told Rebecca.

This was the last thing they needed. It was just days away from the trial.

CHAPTER TWENTY-FOUR

Raj had called Rebecca a few times from prison since the last trial. They had agreed that they could not have frequent contact in case the prosecution got wind of it and used it against Rebecca. The truth was that feelings between them had been woken after they had been thrust together in such extreme circumstances. They had bonded again in a situation that no one else had shared or could completely understand.

Rebecca didn't blame Raj. She knew that he would never have purposely dragged her along. He just didn't think. He always thought he was one step ahead and smarter than the rest. It would never have crossed his mind that anything he did would have an impact on anyone else. He would have thought the same about Suri, his mum and his dad. He would never have intentionally hurt them.

The conversations between them were like they always used to be. It was like one of those friendship where you haven't seen each other for years but it seems like only yesterday. Rebecca was confused. She knew there was no future for them. Her parents, family and friends could not and would not accept them as a couple. Rebecca just couldn't let go though. She wasn't ready to. Not yet.

Raj talked about how he would appeal and get the conviction overturned. His barrister was already working on his grounds to appeal. They felt there had been so many legal errors and points of law wrongly decided during the trial. If

Raj had his conviction quashed or a retrial ordered then this would have a huge impact on Rebecca. If Raj's property was not criminal property then Rebecca could not have knowingly or unknowingly disguised it. Rebecca could not properly be convicted if Raj won his appeal.

Raj seemed hopeful and positive. It was what was keeping him going whilst he was inside. Rebecca noticed the more she spoke to him that he hadn't changed. He was still the same person he was when they were together and it didn't work then. He never took responsibility for his own actions. Everything was always someone else's fault. 'It was because they had done this, he had no choice but to do that.'

Rebecca thought that might have changed when he had actually said sorry for what was happening to her. She realised that this was not the case at all.

'It's my mum and dad's fault,' he told Rebecca on the phone one day angrily. 'They were putting me under pressure about my sister's case so I went to the accountant to sort things out. If they hadn't gone on and on at me, this would never have happened. My sister stopped talking to me. The tax returns and accountant were the only link to me and the money. My barrister told me that. They couldn't have proved criminal property with my sister. There was no link. It's their fault. I snapped at a visit the other day and told them. My mum looked really upset. I had a go. I couldn't help it. It'd been building up in me for ages and I just had to say something.'

Rebecca was shocked. How was this anyone's fault except his own? He could never accept he had done wrong, put his hands up to it and apologise. He had to keep blaming other people. Rebecca had forgotten this side of him when they were in court. It was all starting to come back to her now. She still missed him though. She was still drawn to him. She felt like they were both being victimised. They needed each other... or so she thought.

Raj was so confident about Rebecca's upcoming trial that he made her feel positive about it. He was 100% sure that she would be found not guilty and everything would be OK. He always underestimated things. That was another thing Rebecca had forgotten about him.

Before the trial began, Anne and Peter saw Raj's mother shopping in the town centre. Anne and Peter felt angry with Raj and his whole family. They had sympathy for Suri but still had their reservations about her. They felt that Mr and Mrs Singh were deluded. They hadn't got a clue who their son really was. They thought he was the golden boy. Rebecca felt that they had made him the way he was by treating him like an untouchable. He would never be disciplined by them and would rule the roost at home. Rebecca would cringe whenever she heard him speak to his family. He had no respect or patience with them. Rebecca knew he loved and cared for them but he never ever showed it.

Mrs Singh approached Anne and said hello. Mrs Singh spoke in very broken English and her understanding was very limited. She had always spoken in Punjabi to Raj in front of Rebecca.

'How are you?' Anne asked politely. Anne and Peter were the sort of people that would never be outwardly rude to someone. They would maintain their dignity at all times.

'Yes, yes,' Mrs Singh replied nodding.

Anne could see that this was not the truth. Mrs Singh had aged twenty years in the past few months. They had been regularly referred to as elderly by the prosecution in an attempt to make Raj look like the devil by exploiting them. In fact Mrs Singh was no older than Anne and Peter and much younger than the judge sitting on the trial.

The pressure had taken its toll yet Rebecca was still not certain that the severity of the case and its potential impact had been understood by them. Raj's family had always seemed to have a blasé nature. They had sat in court during the trial eating sweets, rustling paper and letting their mobile phones go off. They had been disruptive rather than supportive and had probably caused more damage than good with the jury.

Rebecca wasn't sure whether Raj had told his family to stop coming to court or whether they had just stopped bothering but gradually they came less and less. By the final stages they were not there at all. Rebecca's family and friends filled the public gallery on a daily basis. Raj had no one. Rebecca felt for him but he did not seem bothered in the slightest. It must have occurred to him though... Rebecca knew that he would have noticed it.

'Rebecca is the love of Raj's life,' Mrs Singh told a shocked Anne.

Anne did not want Raj anywhere near her daughter again.

'Your son,' Anne replied through gritted teeth, 'has dragged my daughter through the courts and destroyed her career.'

'But Rebecca is a good girl,' Mrs Singh responded not quite realising the importance of what Anne was saying. 'She has done nothing,'

'I know she hasn't,' Anne jumped in.

'Raj loves her... it's OK. Nothing will happen to her; she is white.'

Anne could not believe her ears. Is that really what they thought this came down to? Anne made her excuses and left the conversation. They really had no understanding of the significance of what was happening. They were on another planet.

At the office, Duncan walked into Rebecca's room at the office.

'If you want the week off before the trial that's fine,' he told her.

'No it's OK,' she replied.

Rebecca was trying to be positive. She wanted to save her holiday for after the trial. She would need a break. She felt OK; she didn't feel like she needed to prepare herself for the trial. She was ready for it. She also wanted to be in the office in case there were any last minute tricks from the prosecution.

Duncan was kind. He had been so supportive right from the investigation. Most employers would have run a mile. Duncan was like a father figure. He genuinely cared about his employees and would help them whenever they needed it. He could be extremely stern and no nonsense in his approach to work but once you needed him he would be an amazing friend. Rebecca knew it had been extremely stressful for him. She knew she didn't tell him enough exactly how much she appreciated it all. But she did. He had defended her from the outset. She wished she would have had the courage to call him when she was first arrested. She trusted him implicitly and felt safe in his hands. He was the best boss she could have hoped for but with such an emotionally vested interest she was worried about the pressure it was putting on him. She hated the strain that everyone was under because of her.

On the Friday before her trial was due to start, Rebecca packed up her desk. She put all her belongings into a box and made sure all her cases were up to date and memo'd to others to supervise.

Gordon, the other partner at the firm, came into the room.

'What are you doing?' he asked Rebecca with a puzzled expression.

'Just in case.' She smiled at him.

'Oh God.' Gordon frowned, he looked upset.

Rebecca was just trying to be realistic without being dramatic about things. There's a good chance I might not be coming back here, she thought to herself.

CHAPTER TWENTY-FIVE

Rebecca's second trial was due to take a week. There was a lot less evidence to get through compared to last time and Rebecca was going to be on her own in the dock. The focus would be on her completely. Last time the prosecution's main interest had been Raj and some days Rebecca wasn't even mentioned. This time it would be all about her.

'The case of Rebecca Cate Turner is about to be heard in Court 5.'

Matthew, Duncan, Rebecca and her family all stood up and headed into court. It was like de ja vu. Rebecca had been here just months before.

Preliminary matters had to be dealt with first. The prosecution were only pursuing one of the counts.

Kallow rose to his feet. 'The prosecution want this matter to be left on file for the time being,' he told the judge. 'We will not be offering no evidence at this stage.'

Rebecca knew exactly why this was and the judge did too. They wanted to see how the trial went and if Rebecca were to be acquitted they would then attempt to resurrect the other charge. They wanted a third bite at the cherry. The judge wasn't entertaining it.

'If this matter is not being pursued I can see no reason why no evidence cannot be offered at this stage. It cannot be left to hang over people.'

'Very well,' Kallow smiled insincerely, 'the prosecution offer no evidence on count one.'

'A not guilty verdict will then be recorded,' the judge replied.

Rebecca looked to heaven and thanked God. She couldn't stand the prosecution being so manipulative.

Outside court everyone could see how dishonest they were. Plotting their next move, anything to get their conviction then a theatrical performance in court for the judge and jury. Rebecca felt like clapping at the end of Kallow's submissions. They were nothing more than fantasy. It was hard to hear such lies about herself and just having to remain tight lipped. Kallow was known for his disingenuous and aggressive nature within the profession. He was not well liked. Rebecca had heard people discussing him behind his back.

A new jury was empanelled. It consisted of ten men and two women. Rebecca initially thought this was a good thing as women could be judgemental and bitchy when it came to other females. On reflection she decided men could be harsher and have less emotion about things. Rebecca's case was all about emotions. Rebecca felt worried. Men couldn't relate or empathise with her.

The females in the jury were clearly younger than the males. One was a young Asian girl in traditional dress. She would understand how Asian families worked and how Raj would have kept his family life and Rebecca very separate. Rebecca just hoped that the girl was strong enough to have a voice. The other female was a young white girl. Rebecca guessed late teens or early twenties. There were some quite elderly distinguished men in the jury. Rebecca knew from the outset which one would be the foreman. He was a man in his late 60s with grey hair, a slim build and always dressed impeccably in a tweed suit.

'That man in the jury reminds me of Clarence from It's a wonderful life,' said Auntie Denise. 'I think he's got a kind face. He'll look after you I think. I've got a good feeling about him.'

'Do you think?' Rebecca said hopefully.

'I do,' Denise said with certainty. 'Clarence will sort things out.'

Rebecca hoped she was right.

The prosecution opened the case. It was like a completely different case. No longer were they saying that Rebecca was a mastermind, a gangster's moll who had helped Raj to get away with things for so many years. She was just the girlfriend who must have suspected something was going on.

It was emphasized that Rebecca did not need to suspect that Raj was involved in drugs. She must have just suspected that there was some illegal activity which Raj had made his money from. It was changing the goal posts again and lowering what it was they had to prove.

The opening was a lot softer until Raj was mentioned. A lot of the opening focused on him again, 'exploiting his elderly parents and hoarding £250,000 of drug money'. He was such a prolific offender that he was sentenced in this court to 15 years in custody earlier this year. Kallow was really hamming it up. He wanted Raj to sound as nasty and dangerous as possible. He wanted it to be so obvious to everyone what a nasty person he was that Rebecca must have known.

Rebecca could feel the eyes of the jury turning on her one by one as each new piece of information was given to them. Kallow made her sound like such an unpleasant person who deserved to be punished. It wasn't nice to hear but Rebecca had almost become immune to it. What with the last trial, press coverage and gossip she was used to a daily character assassination. Her family and friends knew different. Rebecca was starting to suspect that the judge knew it too. He was doing his job, following the letter of the law but she could see a softer side to him now Raj wasn't next to her.

The prosecution had made an application to adduce Raj's bad character. This meant not just his conviction for drugs but his previous convictions for violence. Albeit they were minor assaults the prosecution wanted them in for two reasons. Firstly to show that Rebecca knew what sort of person he was and would still stand by him and secondly, to suggest that the violence was to do with drug dealing.

If Raj were a big player in the drug world, as they suggested, he would have had to use violence to control his drug debts and his 'patch'. It came with the territory. Rebecca knew that the conviction for assault was nothing to do with drugs. It was a drunken fight in town. Rebecca had been to court with Raj for support when he had been convicted and sentenced. She had heard the full facts and the victims' evidence. There was no suggestion that there was any issue with drugs despite what the prosecution would like people to believe.

The convictions were not admitted in the first trial. They would have been too prejudicial to Raj's case. He was not here this time and so, although convictions of non-defendants are not automatically admitted, the prosecution said that they were relevant. The judged agreed that they were of probative value.

Rebecca thought that the judge believed that they gave an insight into Raj and Rebecca's relationship. They showed that she would stand by him and support him. That was what the prosecution were saying in this case. There was no doubt about it; the admission of the convictions damaged Rebecca's case. Alongside Raj's drugs conviction and minus the police investigation points it was becoming more and more difficult to run a defence.

The only live witness that the prosecution needed to call this time was the accountant Mr Khan. As in the first trial, he produced the scrap of paper as his exhibit and confirmed to the jury that he had not used, relied upon or taken any notice of the piece of paper. He added that the paper had been given to him by Raj but that Rebecca had not been there.

As he repeated almost identical evidence from the first trial, Rebecca still found it shocking to hear that he did exactly what she had done but that he had gone that step further by submitting actual tax forms. He was a prosecution witness and she was the defendant. Rebecca would have laughed at the irony if it wasn't so tragic.

The interviews were read to the jury with extra edits to block out mention of the other count. It was small sections of a long interview which now seemed disjointed. After DC Carter read the interview out there were no real questions that Matthew could ask. Many of the questions he could ask before about the poor investigation and the assumptions that the police had jumped to were now irrelevant. The prosecution had cut down the defence by dropping the other count.

At the end of the prosecution case, Rebecca and her supporters sat outside court waiting for the case to be called back on. A familiar face walked up the stairs and headed towards Rebecca's group.

Where do I know her from? thought Rebecca to herself.

Rebecca just could not place her. She racked her brains. The lady looked like she was waiting to talk to Rebecca. She kept looking over and smiling. The lady approached.

'Can I talk to you?' she asked Rebecca.

It suddenly hit Rebecca. It was one of the women from the jury of the first trial.

'I just heard that your second trial was going ahead, I had to come. I couldn't believe that they were putting you through it again.'

Rebecca was stunned. She did not know what to say.

'I'm being investigated by my company,' the lady continued, 'for the expenses I submitted from your trial. It just made me think how things can be twisted and how horrific it is to be investigated. I wanted to come and show my support.'

'Thank you.' Rebecca smiled.

Matthew came flying past out of nowhere and summoned Rebecca to a side conference room.

'You cannot be seen to be talking to her,' he warned sternly. 'Not only is it an offence for a jury member to discuss the case, even after it has finished but the prosecution would have a field day if they worked out who she is. They could try and suggest all sorts. For your own good, stay away from her.'

Rebecca nodded. Matthew had never been so stern with Rebecca. She knew he was deadly serious.

Rebecca felt a strange sense of loyalty to the lady. She had never spoken to her before and knew nothing of her but Rebecca admired the lady for actually caring about what is right. She felt rude not being able to speak to the lady but had to heed Matthew's warning.

Peter agreed that he would go and speak to the lady and explain why Rebecca couldn't speak to her. He told her that she was still welcome to come into court but that both her and Rebecca could get into trouble if they talked. The lady seemed shocked but nodded that she understood. She stuck around at a distance until things were called back in. She followed and sat in the public gallery with Rebecca's friends and family.

The defence case began with Rebecca's evidence. Although it would be shorter than the last trial Rebecca knew it would still be gruelling. The prosecution knew what she was going to answer now as they had asked it all before. They had served her last evidence on the defence which meant that they would want to question her on it. Rebecca knew that any discrepancy with her evidence or her interview and they would be on her calling her a liar. Rebecca took a deep breath as she walked across the courtroom. She was as ready as she'd ever be.

Matthew asked Rebecca questions first so that she could put her full side of the story across.

Once again she relived her relationship with Raj, the breakup and her moving on without him. She told the jury the minutia of the how they met, dated and how the relationship soured. She told the jury what she remembered about Suri's investigation and when she learned what was going on. Some of her answers were that she didn't remember. She had been arrested years after the things that she was being asked about. She wasn't sure of dates and didn't want to make things worse for herself by guessing. By the end of her examination in chief Rebecca felt that she given as much information as she could.

I've been honest, she thought to herself. She stuck to what she knew. She felt like it had gone as well as it could have.

'Do you still not believe that Raj was a drug dealer, someone who was concerned in the supply of cocaine and heroin on a large scale?' Kallow mocked.

'No,' Rebecca replied... Here we go again, she thought.

'Even though he was convicted by a unanimous jury in front of this very court?' Kallow went on.

Rebecca couldn't win. Whatever she replied could be used against her. She stuck to her guns. Kallow wasn't being as aggressive as last time. Rebecca was always on her guard waiting for something new to be pulled out of the bag. The thing was that she didn't know what they could be so she couldn't prepare herself. Much of what was said was based on assumptions so she could never second guess what the next assumption could be.

Kallow had changed tack. He did not accuse Rebecca of being an actress this time and although Rebecca was under the same amount of pressure as before she felt far too exhausted to cry. She was drained of energy and her emotions were muted.

Rebecca was asked about how Raj had earned his money. Rebecca told the court about selling cars. She had told the officers in interview that Raj had been working at the new car auction in a nearby town. He had called her from there on a number of occasions after they had split up. He had told her how his job was to drive cars out and round as people bid on them. Rebecca remembered how it worked as she had been to a number of car auctions with Raj when they had been together.

Rebecca tried to give as much detail as possible about when Raj bought and sold cars. She had been there when he had bought cars from the auction and had heard him on the phone to the Auto Trader putting ads in.

When the police had checked this, Auto Trader had no record of adverts registered to Raj. Rebecca was confused. She had heard him. She was certain. Rebecca had also been there when Raj had been to pick up used cars the day later from the auctions. The auction had a record of just a handful of vehicles. Rebecca couldn't explain why this was. She was telling the truth but it looked like she was lying. She wasn't a fool. She knew these things would be checked out. She wouldn't have told the police about them if she didn't think they could be confirmed. Rebecca knew how it seemed. It looked bad for her.

Rebecca saw Kallow whispering to DC Carter during her evidence. DC Carter quietly left the court.

'I've just sent the officer to check with the auction about Raj's employment with them,' Kallow declared.

'Good.' Rebecca nodded. 'Check it out. I want you to.'

Rebecca was 100% certain that she would be proved to be telling the truth. Even after all this time she still trusted what Raj had told her. He said he had worked there for months and had even called her to tell her about who he had seen there on some days.

Kallow asked Rebecca about Raj's previous convictions.

'What sort of a man were you going out with? A man who assaults people?'

'I was aware of his previous assault conviction and that he had gone to prison for it,' she replied. 'He told me that he had been defending himself in a fight and I accepted that. That's what you do when you love someone. You support them through it all. You don't just reject and desert people when they need you the most. It's like my family leaving me.' Rebecca gestured towards her family in the public gallery. As she did so she caught the eye of her Auntie Denise. She paused and took a breath to stop the tears coming.

Kallow used this to his advantage.

'So you supported Raj when he was in trouble. Just like you did here. You helped his sister.'

'No,' explained Rebecca. 'I wasn't in a relationship with him when Suri was arrested but I was when he was in trouble. Raj wasn't in trouble here, it was Suri and I had no relationship with her.'

Rebecca knew whatever she answered could be interpreted differently. It wasn't good that the jury saw Raj as a violent man... the association was definitely something that would rub off on to people's views of her.

The cross examination continued. Rebecca knew that a lot of what she was saying hadn't checked out from the first trial. She wasn't about to change her account though. The prosecution didn't have to ask Rebecca about her finances this time. Her bank accounts were of no relevance this time. The cross examination was all about that piece of paper and what she knew at the time. Rebecca was adamant that she did not know about Suri's case when she was helping Raj to fill in his tax return. The prosecution suggested that this was unlikely due to the closeness of her relationship with Raj at the time. They didn't get their relationship at all and they didn't want to.

Rebecca saw DC Carter scurry back into court. Rebecca could see by her eager face that it would mean bad news for her. She saw the officer whisper into the ear of Kallow and his face turn into a smirk as he took in what she was saying.

'Your honour,' he pronounced, 'we have a statement from British Auctions where Ms Turner suggested that Raj Singh worked for a period of time.'

Kallow passed the statement to Matthew. Matthew read it, nodded and handed it back. He gave a half smile to Rebecca as he looked over to the box.

'We have no record of a Mr Singh working for us since 2005 when we opened. He could have been working through an agency but we have stopped using agency recruits since 2009. We would only employ agency workers for a maximum of two months at a time,' Kallow read.

'No!' Rebecca shouted across the court. She could not stop herself. 'That's not true!' she continued. She burst into tears of frustration. She was telling the truth. He did work there. She just looked like complete liar in front of the jury. Her reaction was completely natural; it had made her lose her composure for just a second in front of the jury. It didn't even cross Rebecca's mind that the statement might be true. She was certain it was wrong.

The rest of the cross examination went by in a blur. Had too much damage been done? How could nothing that Rebecca had said have checked out? She couldn't understand it. It was like she was in a bad dream. Rebecca saw the expressions of the jury though. They didn't believe her. She needed her witnesses to back her up and support what she said.

Matthew tried to manage the damage in re-examination by clarifying that Raj could have worked as an agency worker at the auction. Rebecca did not know how he was employed but that he was working there for months. She never asked him how he got his job. Rebecca was so relieved to get down from the box. She looked over at her family who smiled reassuringly but she knew they had felt the blow too.

Raj called Rebecca that night to ask her how things were going. She told him about the statement from the auction.

'I worked there through an agency,' he told her.

He described where the agency was based and gave her details of who to contact to clarify things.

'It doesn't matter,' she told him. 'It's too late now, I've given my evidence. Why weren't there any records of you advertising in Auto Trader? I've heard you on the phone to them?'

'No you've heard me on the phone speaking to a seller from the Auto Trader. I never actually advertise through them. I just used to buy through them.'

Rebecca was confused. That wasn't how she remembered it. It was all so long ago now. She was being honest, as honest as her memory allowed her to be.

These were all things that Rebecca had never asked Raj about during the first trial. They had never come up before and because Raj didn't give evidence she did not hear his explanation for things. It was too late to correct things in her evidence.

'You'll be fine,' Raj told her yet again as they ended their call. Rebecca knew that he really did believe that.

The following day in court the defence case continued. Rebecca did not have to call Nicola, Anita or Annette to give evidence as most of what they said was connected to Rebecca's finances and her role as the group's social organiser.

'I just want your mum and dad, sister and one friend... Jennifer this time,' Matthew informed Rebecca. 'They are just going to confirm the relationship between you and Raj and also what you thought he did. Duncan has managed to persuade Suri to come this afternoon. The prosecution are expecting her this time though so it won't have quite the same impact as last time.' Rebecca nodded.

The defence had lost their element of surprise and the prosecution had had the opportunity to iron out any creases.

Rebecca sat in the dock and watched as the closest people to her were put through an agonising series of questions for a second time. As always, Matthew asked questions first and was followed by the prosecution. The prosecution knew what each witness would say this time so they picked their questions carefully so as to not step into territory that they did not want the jury to know about.

Anne was up first. Rebecca just wanted to cry as she heard her mother read the oath. Why was everyone having to go through this ordeal? Her parents were the most honest, genuine and caring people you would ever meet. Rebecca often thought that people like them did not exist anymore. They were selfless. They were the two people on this earth that did not deserve to be going through this. They had lived their lives abiding by and respecting the law. Rebecca knew that the respect they had had been completely destroyed by the case. She felt saddened by that. It was common for law-abiding citizens to be entangled with the law and to be horrified at what actually goes on. It's only when people are caught in something that their eyes become well and truly opened.

Anne told the court how Rebecca and Raj's relationship was not as serious as was made out. She never saw a future in it. She told how she had only met Raj a handful of times. The problem was that Anne's evidence was again manipulated into looking as though Rebecca had hidden things from her family and friends. That made her look suspicious. Instead of trying to break Anne's evidence, the prosecution's tactic was to accept her as an honest witness but that was because she was lied to by Rebecca. It was obvious that Rebecca's witnesses were genuine and so the prosecution stopped trying to discredit them like in the first trial. The jury hadn't liked that before and it had gone against Kallow and his sidekick. There were only a few questions asked of Anne by Kallow.

Peter was called. Rebecca saw again how nervous her dad was. Matthew tried to show another side of Rebecca through Peter by asking about her character. Rebecca could see Peter's pride as he spoke of his daughter and described her as a strong-willed little girl. It broke Rebecca's heart to see that her dad was still proud of her despite where she was sitting.

Kallow kept the cross examination short. The more questions they were asked the more the jury liked Rebecca's witnesses. The prosecution did not want that.

Marie was next up. She described Rebecca as always crying when she was with Raj. This made Marie burst into tears as she remembered how distressed her sister was. She recalled that she did not like Raj. Kallow did not ask Marie any questions at all. Rebecca could see the relief in Marie's face as she stepped down from the witness box.

Jennifer's evidence was similar to Marie's. Once again Kallow decided not to cross examine Jennifer. It didn't really seem to matter if the jury believed Rebecca's witnesses or not. They could be truthful but Rebecca could have fed them a pack of lies.

After lunch, Suri arrived. Rebecca hadn't seen her since the first trial. She was grateful that she hadn't backed out. She had no loyalty to Rebecca, they barely knew one another.

As Suri walked into the courtroom she could see that the jury were interested in Suri and what she had to say. They had heard her name constantly for the last week and now they were going to hear directly from her. Suri confirmed that she barely knew Rebecca and that she had not spoken to her about her case at any time. She was also adamant that Raj was not a drug dealer. Matthew asked Suri if Raj had worked at the auction and she confirmed that he had but did not know any more detail than that. She couldn't say if it was through an agency. Suri was a helpful witness. She came across as articulate and smart. Rebecca couldn't tell if the jury liked her or not.

Kallow was harsh with his questioning of Suri. He accused her of lying about her brother. He did not seem to focus on what Suri had said about Rebecca but more so on the truth about Raj. Suri became upset as her word was questioned. She sobbed as she told the court that she would not swear to God and then lie. She had strong religious beliefs. As she was discharged as a witness she ran out of court and flung the door open in floods of tears. She was clearly insulted and upset at how Kallow had tried to portray her.

Rebecca left court and saw Anne with her arm around Suri outside. Suri was sobbing and just kept on repeating,

'He said I lied when I swore to God.'

She was so upset that everyone was upset for her. Rebecca looked up as she sat down next to Suri and saw the lady from the first jury looking over and watching from across the foyer. She too looked upset. This was the reality. The courtroom was just acting and games, a platform for the prosecution to put on their play while the defence fought for their lives.

After Suri, the defence case had closed. It was just left for each side to make their speeches to the jury and for the judge to sum up all the evidence and direct the jury accordingly.

The prosecution allegation had become lower and lower throughout the trial. They did not uphold that they thought Rebecca knew all about the drugs and Raj's 'business ventures'. They were settling for 'she's a clever girl, she must have suspected something was dodgy when she wrote on that piece of paper.'

Rebecca had to admit if she had watched the prosecution case before Raj had come round that night she probably would have been suspicious, but things don't happen like that in real life. Things aren't always that obvious.

Matthew did a good job when it came to his turn to speak. He wasn't lost under mountains of bank statements, financial documents and other paperwork this time.

Finally it was the judge's turn to sum things up. Rebecca thought he was fair generally. He focused on a part of Rebecca's interview that the prosecution had emphasized in both of the trials. He read the part about Rebecca saying 'she had shown it to me' meaning the paperwork from Suri's case.

They took that to mean Suri. But both Rebecca and Suri confirmed in their evidence that they had never discussed the case. Kallow fixated on the word 'she'. In truth, Rebecca couldn't account for why she had said she. She was under extreme pressure in a police interview. It must have been a slip of the tongue. As she went on in the interview she confirmed that she had never spoken to Suri about it. Rebecca wasn't even sure that she had said she. If she had said it she didn't mean it. She couldn't even recall what she had been shown by Raj when he eventually told her about Suri's case. It all seemed so irrelevant at the time. She couldn't be certain if he'd ever actually shown her anything at all.

The way the judge read the passage Rebecca knew she was in trouble. The things she had said in interview had been shown to be unreliable. The jury didn't buy her story. Rebecca usually had a sense, a gut feeling as to if something was going to be OK or not. She didn't have that feeling this time. There was nothing she could do. It was in the hands of the jury.

The jury was sent out to reach a verdict. Rebecca was scared. A very different picture had been painted of her. The first trial was a full picture but this one was a snapshot that had been created by the prosecution. By dropping the first count they had excluded a lot, all of which had been favourable to Rebecca. Rebecca didn't think that she had had a fair trial but what is fair and what is seen as fair by the law are two very different things.

The excruciating waiting began again. Everyone important in Rebecca's life, family and friends, were there with her. It would have been lovely if it wasn't for the reason behind the meeting.

After a couple of hours, the jury were discharged for the day. Rebecca was still as jumpy as ever but she didn't think the jury would be too quick to come back. The last one had taken its time and she hoped that her case wasn't quite so cut and dry.

Another sleepless night, another trip back to Anne and Peter's. There were so many of Rebecca's family that they couldn't all be put up. They had started staying in the hotel close to the court. The case was draining people, financially, emotionally and mentally.

They trooped up to court the following morning and waited as the jury reconvened their deliberations. After a couple of hours Rebecca heard her case being called to the courtroom. She stood up and as her friends and family walked in; she was left at the back with Marie and Anne.

'I'm scared,' she told them as tears dripped down her face.

'Come on,' Anne said sternly putting her arms around Rebecca's shoulders. 'You're going to be alright.' Anne wiped Rebecca's tears away. 'It's nearly over,' she told her. 'Be strong.'

Rebecca nodded. She did not want to show the officers waiting in court that they had got to her. She did not want them to have the satisfaction.

Rebecca made her way to the dock. Matthew turned and mouthed, 'It's a verdict,' to her.

Rebecca exhaled through her nose and closed her eyes. Ready or not it was about to happen. Rebecca couldn't stop her tears, they streamed down her face.

The next two minutes will change my life forever, she thought.

The judge entered and the jury swarmed in.

'Can the defendant stand,' the clerk ordered.

'Have you reached a verdict on which you are all agreed?'

'Yes,' replied the foreman.

The foreman was Clarence, Rebecca's guardian angel, but Rebecca didn't get a good vibe from him.

'On the charge of disguising criminal property how do you find the defendant?'

'Guilty.'

Rebecca immediately stopped crying. It was over. There was a chorus of gasps from the public gallery and other shouts of 'no.'

Rebecca heard Anne's voice. 'Bastards,' she scolded. It was the first and only time Rebecca had heard Anne swear.

Rebecca looked up. She saw the two young girls in the jury crying. Why are you crying? she thought. They had a voice in there. Why didn't they use it?

Rebecca turned to the front and saw the elderly usher had tears down her face. She had sat in on both trials and had seen both cases from start to finish. The judge looked visibly shocked.

Rebecca sat down as the jury walked out. Their heads were held down. Not one of them could look her in the eye after what they had just done.

'If I was sure that someone was guilty of something I could hold my head up high and look them in the eye.'

The jury left looking ashamed of themselves.

And so you should be, Rebecca thought.

As soon as the verdict came in Rebecca felt angry. Her fear and upset disappeared in an instant. She would deal with whatever sentence they threw at her now. It was the conviction that mattered to her; to her the sentence was irrelevant. She wasn't afraid of that.

In the blink of an eye she had just lost her job, her career, her home, her financial stability and what was left of her battered reputation.

The case was adjourned for a week for sentence. The judge wanted time to consider things. He wasn't ready to sentence Rebecca straight away.

Rebecca left the dock, as she was released by the guard, she looked at her with sympathy.

'I'm not supposed to say this but I just can't believe it,' she told Rebecca.

Why couldn't the jury see what others could? Rebecca wondered.

Rebecca went into a conference room with Duncan, Matthew and her parents. She left her family and friends in floods of tears outside the courtroom. Everyone was devastated.

'I'm so sorry Rebecca.' Duncan's voice broke as he gulped back tears.

'It's not your fault,' she told him. 'Thank you for everything. You did everything you could for me.'

The rest of the conference was just a blur. Matthew could see that Rebecca was just in a daze. She wasn't emotional, she actually felt a strong sense of relief that it was actually over. Although it was the verdict that she had dreaded, she knew what she was dealing with now. She could cope. She knew she could. She was strong and she was not going to let them destroy her.

Months after the verdict, Rebecca saw online that Kallow had been made a QC. She could have almost laughed. That was probably why he was so smug. He'd made his name with her case and used it to further his career. Her faith, what little she still had in the justice system, diminished further as she learnt that who would be considered the crème de la crème of the legal world was in fact a devious, manipulative man.

CHAPTER TWENTY-SIX

After the verdict Rebecca started getting things prepared ready for her sentence. She had had to hand in her resignation to Duncan. Rebecca was told by her closest friend at work, Janine, that some of her colleagues had burst into tears.

'We don't care what the verdict said, we stand by Rebecca 100%.' Everyone nodded in agreement. Duncan had advised them not to contact Rebecca for a day or two while things sank in. Janine didn't listen, she was so close to Rebecca that she knew she had to call.

Rebecca was surprisingly upbeat when she answered.

'Idiots,' she said referring to the jury. 'Oh well. I'll just have to deal with whatever it is that they throw at me. I'm ready for it,' she told Janine, 'I genuinely am.'

Rebecca was being honest. She didn't need to lie to Janine about anything.

Bring it on, she thought.

The next week was spent arranging viewings of Rebecca's house to rent out, authorising Anne and Peter to make decisions on her bank account and allowing them to represent her interests in connection to the house. Rebecca didn't know whether she would be going into custody or not. She did not want to leave an empty house with a mortgage to pay for her parents to deal with. It wouldn't be fair on top of everything else they were dealing with.

Anyway Rebecca would not have wanted to continue to live there regardless of her sentence. She wanted to get away for a while and relocate. That place had too many bad memories. The police banging on the door and searching through her private things, Raj turning up at the door asking questions, his junkie brother walking past every five minutes. These were things Rebecca wanted to forget about completely.

The plan was that if she was not sent to prison she would move up north with her parents in Lancashire. She had no friends there but she knew she already had strong friendships that would survive the distance. Her cousins were about the same age as Rebecca and lived only 30 minutes away from Anne and Peter's. She could re-start her life without thinking that everyone was talking about her or living in fear that the police would come knocking again.

Rebecca hadn't really slept since that November morning. She constantly had flashbacks of those heavy thuds at the door. Even though she'd handled it at the time there was still fear that it would happen again. Rebecca was paranoid that they would want to talk to her about something again. It was irrational and she knew it was but it was a feeling that she had to fight away often. She'd always been a light sleeper but now she woke at the slightest sound. It was like some kind of post-traumatic stress.

Raj called Rebecca the night the jury came back with their verdict.

'Guilty,' she told him.

He thought she was joking. 'I swear.' He couldn't believe it.

'Well I'm going to get my appeal and then that'll change things,' he tried to reassure her. 'You've got to appeal,' he encouraged.

'No,' she told him. 'I don't want to. My family have been through enough. I want to move on and we can't do that with an appeal hanging over us. I want it over.'

Rebecca had already made up her mind. Peter had been asking Matthew about an appeal in the conference room after her conviction. She had said then that she didn't want to. They had obviously thought she was still in shock but she had made her mind up before the verdict was delivered. Raj was supportive of Rebecca, saying all the right things. She could tell he was upset. He didn't tell her he was sorry for it all but Rebecca still didn't blame him. She wasn't mad or angry with him. Everyone else was and she knew they'd never ever forgive him for what had happened.

'Oh yes, one other thing,' she told him, 'my sentence date. It's on your birthday.'

CHAPTER TWENTY-SEVEN

It was the day of sentence. Rebecca walked into the courthouse with her head held high. She was angry with the prosecutors, the police and the jury. She had nothing to be ashamed of, they should be embarrassed for being a part of what had happened. She wheeled her large holdall bag up the ramp. It was packed with everything she might need in prison. She was ready to go if that was what the judge wanted. She wasn't going to shed any more tears or waste any more time worrying about this. It had already taken up 18 months of her life. Rebecca did not want to go to prison for the sake of her family and friends. She did not know how they would cope with all the worry. She wanted it to end for them today but with a prison sentence it would continue until her release.

As she stood outside the courtroom Matthew came and spoke to her about the procedure for today. She tried to crack a joke. In hindsight it was probably not appropriate in the circumstances. Matthew snapped. Rebecca had never seen him so stressed. She knew he was under immense pressure today to keep her out.

Every single person who was important to Rebecca was in that courtroom. The public gallery was so full that her family and friends had to sit in the press section and some had to stand at the back. Rebecca marched into court defiantly. She felt furious that she was there. The judge entered and everyone was seated as Rebecca was asked to confirm her identity. She did so with venom in her voice. She saw DC Moran at the corner of the court. She stared at him intensely. She hated him. He hadn't believed her from the start. Maybe if he'd just checked her story about the money she would have never even got to court. She didn't feel like they were just doing their jobs. She honestly felt that they were being malicious. It was a witch hunt because she was a defence solicitor and they saw her as the enemy. It was a victory for them. She despised them all.

'You may be seated,' the judge told Rebecca. 'What I have to say may take some time. Now I want to say straight away that I am not going to sentence you to an immediate custodial sentence today.'

There was a huge sigh of relief from the public gallery followed by tears. Rebecca could see Marie sobbing in the arms of Peter. Marie had never told Rebecca how scared she was for her but her reaction had just made it clear. Rebecca looked over at her friends with tissues wiping their eyes. It made her more and more angry. Every single one of them didn't deserve to be put through this. Rebecca felt like it was her fault for being with Raj and she felt guilty. She knew she hadn't broken the law and she shouldn't be here. She'd been punished enough through her relationship with him.

'I wanted to say that at the outset as I can see the stress and pressure you have all been under,' the judge continued as he looked at the public gallery.

He can see what sort of people my family and friends are, Rebecca thought. He has empathy with them.

In order to give a suspended sentence the judge had to give exceptional circumstances why the suspension should be put in place rather than activated immediately.

The judge explained that Rebecca had been through two trials and the stress, pressure and wait for them must have been excruciating and a punishment in itself.

He added that Rebecca was of good character, had a good reputation and talent in her career and that this would now be taken from her. He added that he hoped she would be able to practice again and that she would not be prevented from doing so forever.

He accepted the references that had been provided during the trial and noted them.

He called Rebecca a fool. The judge did not think that she had been involved with or aware of anything to do with drugs and noted that had he thought that she would have been looking at an immediate custodial sentence of around four years. The judge stated that an important part of the case had been Rebecca's inability to say no to Raj. He stated that this was illustrated by her getting back together with him so easily each time.

That wasn't exactly true. Rebecca had made the final break and moved on from Raj. They hadn't been together for years before the trial. That was neither here nor there now. The verdict had been decided.

It was clear from the sentencing remarks that the judge liked Rebecca and her family. The only negative comment was that she was a fool who would do anything for Raj.

The sentence imposed was one of nine months imprisonment suspended for 18 months with 200 hours unpaid work. He also fined Rebecca £5000 with a surcharge of £15 and prosecution costs of £3000. This had to be paid within six months or Rebecca would receive three months in custody.

Initially, Rebecca was angry with the financial penalty. She had just lost her job and her prospects. How could she even start to pay it? The judge knew that her family had money as it had been apparent during the trial. He must have known that they would have to pay it.

There was no way they'd let her go to prison for three months.

In retrospect, Rebecca could see that he had to give the harshest sentence possible without immediate custody so that it could not be appealed for being too lenient. It took her a good few months to fully understand that.

Outside court Rebecca was still ranting about the fine. Matthew must have thought she was so ungrateful. She should be pleased she's not leaving in a prison van he must have thought.

Suddenly there was nothing more to say. It was all over. Rebecca thanked Matthew and Duncan and left court with plans to rebuild her life starting from scratch.

Raj called Rebecca that afternoon. He seemed reasonably pleased with the sentence but told Rebecca he 'knew you would never go to prison'. He never could see how serious it all was. Rebecca thought back to when she was first arrested and he told her that nothing was going to happen. He had no idea the effect this had had on everyone involved. He wasn't stupid but it was as though he had no comprehension of the seriousness of it all. To him it seemed no big deal.

Rebecca was in the national papers the following day. The headline was 'solicitor hides heroin stash'. Rebecca just sighed. It was a completely inaccurate and poisonous account.

Online people had commented how she should have gone to prison and that she had only got off so lightly because she was a woman.

There are a lot of ignorant people in the world, Rebecca thought. They believe everything they read and form a strong opinion on it without knowing the full facts.

The photograph attached was obviously taken off guard as she walked into the court building. It was very unflattering. Rebecca felt more upset about that than the article itself. She had thicker skin now.

The house was bought by the first family who were shown around. Rebecca was relieved it was off her hands. It was one less thing to think about and one less link to the past.

Rebecca had one last night out with her friends before all her things were moved up to her parents. They met up for a goodbye drink. It was sad that it had come to this and that she felt that she had to leave people that she cared so much about.

Meanwhile the calls between her and Raj continued and became more frequent. At first Rebecca looked forward to his calls. She missed him and wanted to hear his voice. As time passed she felt guiltier and guiltier about how her family would feel if they knew. They would feel so let down. She told Raj how she felt. They would never accept him being in her life. Once again he had that hold over her. He was in prison and she felt like she couldn't desert him when he was so vulnerable. She wanted him to suggest that the contact had to stop but she knew deep down that he wouldn't do that because it meant putting her feelings before his. That was something that he had never done. She wasn't quite ready to stop the contact herself.

Rebecca found herself at the job centre for the first time in her life. It was somewhere that she never ever foresaw that she would be. She had no choice. She had a conviction now and she didn't know how long it would take her to find a job. She couldn't work in what she was trained in. At the initial interview the assistant told Rebecca that she was overqualified for many of the jobs that they had on offer. The companies wouldn't like her to be put forward as they knew she would leave as soon as something better came along. They were right of course but that didn't help Rebecca right now.

One thing that Rebecca was determined to do after the trial, no matter what the outcome, was to complain about the officers handling of the case. Peter and Anne were angry too. Their bank accounts had been obtained with a production order and trawled through by police officers. The police had consent to request the documents but hadn't bothered. It was humiliating for Anne and Peter to have that in their banking history.

Peter made a complaint to professional standards at the local police station. They made a polite note of what had been said and told him that as the case was not about him, he would have to complain through Rebecca. The senior officer advised Peter that he would 'have a word' with the officers involved.

They all laughed about the complaints procedure. The first stage is to complain to a department at the same police station, where an officer who knows and works with those who are complained about, decides if there is a valid complaint. Rebecca had to give a statement setting out the grounds of her complaint. She wanted all three officers, Carter, Moran and Simmons, to be looked into. Not one of them had done their job properly in her eyes. As the officer taking the statement was making a note of the names he commented, 'DC Carter? She's lovely I can't see her being malicious with anyone.'

Rebecca just smiled to herself. This was supposed to be an impartial handling by the police... some things never change.

Sure enough months later, Rebecca received a report stating that none of the officers had done anything malicious but that there had been some minor errors during their investigation which could be dealt with by way of a 'talking to' by superiors.

This wasn't enough for Rebecca. She needed them to at least acknowledge that she had been treated unfairly. She had been dragged to hell, friends and family in tow, by these officers. She needed her inner thought to be confirmed by someone. She knew it would have to be someone independent who would have to look at the complaint. The police would never want to criticise themselves, it would leave them open to all sorts of actions against them.

The report accepted that DC Carter had not done her job properly but excused her negligence, which Rebecca felt was deliberate, by stating that the officer had too many other matters to deal with. They offered management dispute resolution which would have no effect on the officers' career, record or opportunities for future promotion. That was what Rebecca needed.

Rebecca was unhappy with the findings. Peter agreed. 'It seems like a complete whitewash to me,' he told her, 'if you can appeal I would.' Anne was much more reluctant. She was afraid that the police would come after Rebecca again if she didn't drop it.

'Why should I?' Rebecca argued with Anne. 'They deserve to be punished for what they did!'

'I just want it to end,' Anne replied tearfully. She was frightened for her daughter.

Rebecca forwarded her complaint to the IPCC. She directed it to the findings on DC Carter. DC Moran and DC Simmons were to be given training and supervision under the initial recommendations. Rebecca doubted that this would actually ever happen. She would never know either way. Her main issue was with Carter, she had had conduct of the case.

DC Carter was questioned under caution. Rebecca was pleased that she would have felt the same fear and anxiety that she felt when she was investigated. Mainly, Rebecca didn't want anyone else to go through what she did unnecessarily. She wanted it logged against the officer so that future investigations could resurrect it.

DC Carter stated that she had not maliciously neglected to carry out her duties on Rebecca's case and that she was concentrating on other cases. She felt that Rebecca was maliciously making this complaint. She denied pointing Rebecca out to the reporter and minimised her behaviour throughout the investigation. She stated that Rebecca had actually been given preferential treatment during her time in custody.

When Rebecca referred her complaint to the IPCC, what Rebecca did not realise was that in fact this only involved the IPCC looking at the report of professional standards and pointing out its failings. It then is referred back to professional standards to correct those errors and reassess the situation. Again this is done by a high ranking police officer. 'How is that independent?!' Rebecca was flabbergasted.

The IPCC asked that reasons be given for DC Carter's failure to contact witnesses, for the officer ignoring documentary evidence and for the passing of the case to the CPS for a charging decision without the investigation being complete. They further requested that DC Carter's bias be questioned as it had not been to date.

Following further 'investigation', the officers' findings were forwarded to the IPCC.

Rebecca received a letter stating that whilst the officer had failed to investigate her case correctly, she had such an excessive case load that it could not be misconduct. From the look of it they had simply asked the officer to list the cases she was working on at the time. Clearly the officer would list a huge amount of cases, Rebecca thought suspiciously. I'll bet that wasn't checked by way of dates and work carried out on relevant days.

The senior officer recommended the Management Sanction but added that the officer's failing should be noted on her annual appraisal.

The senior officer stated that the officer was not at the house searches in the case and therefore it was not her fault that documents assisting the defence, which were right next to documents seized and used, were ignored. Rebecca had already raised that other officers were to blame for this but had been told that as they were not the officer in the case responsibility does not rest with them. 'Everyone just passes the buck.' Rebecca was so fed up.

She read on. The senior officer suggested that the officer learn for the future to refer cases to the CPS once her investigations were completed. They did not find that this particular complaint was upheld as they felt it made no difference to the case as a whole. 'Unbelievable!! How can they say that!?' Rebecca believed that if they had spoken to her witnesses they would have supported and proved her defence just like it happened at trial. 'Of course that would have made a difference! What a joke!' She was fuming. She wanted to stop reading. She wondered why she had even thought this would be fair.

Finally the report detailed the findings on whether or not they felt DC Carter was malicious.

The senior officer felt that Carter had carried out a credible investigation and that there had been operational failings rather than a vendetta.

It seemed to Rebecca that what she said in interview was doubted and questioned but what Carter had said was taken as gospel and accepted. Rebecca knew it had been personal with Carter. No report would convince her any different.

Rebecca had 28 days to decide if she wanted to appeal again to the IPCC. She did. She was going to go as far as she could with this. She sent her appeal off and waited.

Months later Rebecca received her response. She was told by the IPCC that their role was only to review the investigation into her complaint and not the complaint itself. Their decision is final unless matters are taken to the courts for judicial review which would be a costly exercise. That was not an option for Rebecca.

Rebecca read her report. They found that the investigation was carried out properly but not in the amount of depth that Rebecca had wanted. Rebecca had wanted a review of the departmental resourcing and responsibilities. She did not accept that the officer's word about how busy she had been was good enough.

The IPCC found that there had been organisational failures rather than bias. Rebecca did not agree.

She was disappointed with the whole system. 'A complaint is made about the police to the police, then reviewed by ex- police officers now working for the IPCC. There was nothing independent about it,' she told Anne and Peter. Rebecca was comforted by the fact that records would now be kept of DC Carter's work and she hoped the officer would think twice before treating anyone in the same way.

After settling in up north with her parents, Rebecca started her unpaid work at a charity shop. She got to know the volunteers and staff there. She enjoyed meeting and spending time with different people. They were all ages from all walks of life. These people became her friends. They often spent staff nights out drinking together. Some people knew why Rebecca was there but others that she told couldn't quite understand why what she did was wrong. It was hard to explain and Rebecca sometimes felt that people thought she was holding things back or lying because it all sounded so ridiculous. She completed her 200 hours over six months and had glowing references from the manager at the store. She enjoyed her time there so much so that she continued to go in every week to help out as a volunteer.

The fine had been paid shortly after the sentencing hearing. Rebecca's family had given her the cash and insisted that she take it down to the court to pay it in immediately. They just wanted it over and done with. Rebecca was so grateful. She would have struggled to come up with that sort of money in such a short space of time. It was yet another unbelievable gesture from her family. She couldn't have coped without them.

When a person is convicted of an offence many issues arise as a result. These are mostly things that people don't even think of at the time. Insurance of any kind is almost impossible to get. Rebecca had to ring round endless insurance companies to get her car insured to drive. As soon as she told people she had been convicted of money laundering they wouldn't touch her with a barge pole.

Finally, Rebecca found one company that would cover the uninsurable. The premiums were doubled but she had no option. It was pay out or no car.

She had also wanted to go on holiday. She needed a break to relax. Her cousin had invited her to USA for a road trip she had planned. Rebecca had to apply for a visa. She couldn't get in as normal now she had a conviction. This meant endless application forms, huge administration fees and a visit to the embassy where she was interviewed. Rebecca had prepared a bundle for her interview and taken extracts from the case as well as references. She explained to the interviewer fully about the allegation, her conviction and the sentence. She showed all the transcripts and paperwork to support her.

'You poor thing. What a nightmare,' the lady exclaimed. 'Usually this sort of offence you are ineligible but I am suggesting we waive this in the circumstances and allow you in.' Rebecca smiled. 'But,' the lady added, 'it has to go to one other agency who will see my recommendation but will make the final decision.'

Rebecca was over the moon. She didn't expect anything when she applied after reading the strict guidelines on the embassy website.

Rebecca had to wait six months before she got her decision. Her visa was refused. She was crushed. She would never be able to put things behind her. They would always affect her and this was just another reminder of that. Rebecca had come to realise that some people had empathy for her and others thought she got what she deserved. It was the same everywhere she went. 'You shouldn't have been so stupid and naive.'

After continuously looking, Rebecca found a job where she could work from her parents' home. She would be completing research and analysis for a computer company. Rebecca felt so lucky to have got the job. The salary was enough for her to live on and cover her debts. It had been one of Rebecca's worries that she would only ever be able to find a job with a much lower wage. Once again Rebecca had been helped by her family. Her uncle had put her in touch with someone he knew and put in a good word for her. Working from home was something that Rebecca had always dreamed of doing. It seemed like things were finally coming together and she was getting her life, a new life, on track.

CHAPTER TWENTY-EIGHT

A letter dropped through the door for Rebecca. It was from the Solicitors Regulation Authority asking her to account for her behaviour. They needed to decide whether Rebecca should be sent to the disciplinary tribunal. At that moment in time Rebecca never wanted to work as a solicitor again. She would have felt so vulnerable being in that position again. She didn't want to give anyone that same kind of power that they had over her again.

Rebecca sent a strong letter back stating in no uncertain terms that she did not intend to practice as a solicitor again and therefore felt no need to be referred to a tribunal. She stated that she accepted that she had been convicted of an offence, that she could not deny, but she did not accept that she was actually guilty of the offence.

Going to the tribunal would mean most costs that Rebecca would be bound to have to cover. She had had quite enough of being in front of tribunals while people judged and made decisions on her future. She did not want to be a solicitor. Why couldn't they just leave it at that? Rebecca hoped they would.

Rebecca slowly started to feel like herself again. She based herself away at her parents' house but would visit her friends when she needed to. They all came to visit her for weekends. Rebecca felt a lot safer at her parents. She felt anonymous rather than 'that solicitor'.

She started socialising at weekends with her cousin and her friendship group. They were all so friendly they soon felt like a true part of the group. Her cousin, Yvonne, was a big part in bringing Rebecca back to life. They spent a lot of time together. She wasn't just her cousin she became one of her best friends.

Rebecca tried to lessen the contact with Raj. The guilt she felt each time he rang increased and she realised that he would never stop calling of his own accord. She kept putting off speaking to him about it; it was Christmas, he was waiting for his appeal, it was her birthday, it was his. It was excuse after excuse. She knew she had to do it but even though it was the right thing to do for everyone involved, she hated the fact that she was hurting him. She still cared about him and it hurt her to upset him.

After Rebecca discovered she couldn't go away to USA, Yvonne suggested they go to Thailand together for the whole summer. Rebecca thought it was a great idea. She made arrangements with work to book time off and saved her wages. Rebecca knew she had to break the news to Raj that they could never be together and they had to cut contact to save each other's feelings. She decided she was going to do it before she went away.

'There's always going to be an event, something for you to blame to put it off,' Anita told her. 'You have to put yourself first now. What do you want?'

'I care about him but I cannot and will not put my family through anything else. They have been through too much and been so supportive,' Rebecca replied.

'Well you know what you have to do?' Anita told her... 'Just do it.'

As Rebecca built up to make the break, she started to be mean and off with Raj on the phone. She couldn't help it. She knew it wasn't fair on him. She was his lifeline on the outside. She helped to keep him going. She had so many battles with her heart and her head. She was dreading it. She cried every time she got off the phone, she felt so guilty. She just wanted to be out of the situation.

Around this time Rebecca received a letter from the Solicitors Regulation Authority telling her that she was to go to London for the tribunal to hear her case. It advised that she could seek representation to assist.

More costs, she thought.

Rebecca expected to be struck off the role of solicitors and be told never to practice again. She had seen in the law gazette pages and pages of cases of solicitors who had got in trouble. That would be her, thousands and thousands of solicitors will be reading about me all over the UK. Rebecca did not have to attend the hearing. It could be done in her absence. She went downstairs and spoke to Anne and Peter.

'You have to go,' they told her. 'You have to go and defend yourself.'

'What's the point?' Rebecca asked them. 'I'll just be struck off. It doesn't matter what I say so what's the point in wasting time and money going down there?'

'I think you should go,' Anne reassured her.

Rebecca listened to her parents reluctantly and filled in the form confirming that she would be there. The added stress and pressure gave Rebecca the strength to finally tell Raj how she felt. She was honest with him. She told him that he would never be accepted by her family and friends. Raj finally understood.

'Well I won't call again then,' he told her but asking it as a question.

'OK,' she answered. She could tell Raj wanted her to fight for him but there was nothing left in her.

'I love you,' he told her as he ended the call.

'I love you too,' she replied.

Rebecca received an email months later. It contained updates on recent case law. She had signed up when she was practising as often there were helpful cases that she could cite in court.

Rebecca's eye was drawn to the case of R v Singh. It was Raj. It listed his grounds for appeal against conviction and sentence. Rebecca noted that he had appealed on the basis of wrongly admitted evidence including the previous convictions of others that Raj had associated with.

Rebecca scrolled down to the decision... Leave to appeal was not granted. Rebecca felt sad for Raj. She knew that that was keeping him going in there. Focusing on getting out earlier than planned and living for that next legal decision. She also felt relieved though. She wouldn't have to deal with the repercussions of the decision and pick up the pieces like she used to do. A huge weight had been lifted off her shoulders when she had stopped contact with Raj. She felt free.

Thailand came at the right time. Rebecca needed a long break to forget about Raj and put the tribunal to the back of her mind.

The trip was a holiday of a lifetime. Rebecca felt completely happy for the first time in years. She felt back to her old self. She loved every minute of it. She'd never been anywhere quite like it. It was like a different world. She had so much fun with Yvonne and met people from all over the world. Rebecca felt fixed.

She had been at her parents for 18 months by the time she returned from Thailand. She realised that as much as she had grown so close to her parents and no matter how much she enjoyed her nights out with Yvonne, she missed Marie and her old friends. Rebecca felt ready to go back.

She flew back into Heathrow and decided to spend a few days with Marie. Rebecca made plans with Nicola to go round to her house and meet up with a few old friends. As everyone arrived, Rebecca saw Steve walking up the path. She had known Steve for years and had always got on really well with him. She always knew he had a soft spot for her but had never looked at him like that. She'd always been too preoccupied. Rebecca heard Nicola's boyfriend let Steve in. He walked into the lounge and immediately there was something different about him. It was like there was an instant connection between them and Rebecca knew something had changed.

'Hi, babe.' He smiled at her. He leant over and kissed Rebecca on the cheek. They both smiled at each other.

The group had a few drinks at Nicola's house before heading on to a pub. On the way Steve spoke to Rebecca about Raj.

'We don't speak to each other anymore,' Rebecca told him. It was true. She hadn't heard from him for months now.

'It's for the best,' Steve told her. She loved that she had no worries with Steve about having to explain her past. He knew what had happened and he didn't judge her. They chatted, laughed and joked for most of the night. She loved his company and for the first time she realised she liked him... a lot.

At the end of the night he leant in to kiss her goodbye and it was electric. She knew the kiss was the start of something special. It was the first time she had felt so happy with herself for such a long time. It could have happened years ago between them but the timing now was perfect. It was meant to be.

Nicola told Rebecca after as she gushed about Steve, 'We could all see it a mile off. It's being coming for a long time with you two. For him, it's always been all about you.'

Rebecca couldn't be happier.

Rebecca went back up north but spent hours on the phone with Steve every night. It felt so natural with them. Rebecca felt the excitement and the butterflies every time she saw his name flash up on her phone. Rebecca started to come down more regularly to see Steve. She drove down most weekends so that they could spend time together. She started to feel even more determined to come back. She felt alive again.

CHAPTER TWENTY-NINE

The day for the disciplinary tribunal had arrived. Anne and Peter had arranged to fly down to support Rebecca. Rebecca didn't hold out much hope. She expected to be struck off or, at least, years of suspension.

I'll never practice as a solicitor again, she thought to herself.

As Rebecca travelled down to London for the hearing, she ran over and over what she planned to say. She was glad that she hadn't just accepted being removed from the roll. Things had changed since last year and she wanted the choice to work as a solicitor if she ever felt ready to do so again. She had worked hard to qualify and she didn't want it to be all for nothing.

Anne and Peter hugged Rebecca as they met outside the Law Society. The two people she could always rely on. Steve called Rebecca to wish her luck.

'I hope they see the sort of person you really are,' he told her.

As they were called in Rebecca scanned the room. It looked just like a magistrate's court, with a clerk, a prosecutor and three lay people on the tribunal. Rebecca spoke to the prosecutor beforehand. She confirmed that she would have to accept that she had called the profession into disrepute by virtue of her conviction. She discussed the costs that Rebecca would have to pay.

More money, she thought. They agreed that the costs would be £2000.

'£10,000 all together with the court fines, that will be. £10,000 for dating a rogue.' Rebecca shook her head.

The tribunal entered and the hearing began. The prosecutor set out the facts and explained Rebecca's conviction. He was fair and accurate. There were no theatrics, it was based completely on the facts. It was then Rebecca's turn. She stood up and cleared her throat. It was the first time she had spoken in front of people since the trial. She was nervous. She took a deep breath and explained the background to her trial. Duncan had provided her with a glowing reference which had also included his take on the trial. She felt emotional as she explained how much she had lost and pleaded with them to consider allowing her to practice again. Rebecca had brought the transcript of the judge's comments from her sentencing. She drew the tribunal's attention to his description of her, what she had been found guilty of doing and his hope that she should practice again.

It was hard for Rebecca to hold it together and as she spoke about things all the emotions came rushing back. She fought back the tears as she thanked the tribunal and sat down. She had done her best. It was out of her hands now.

Before retiring the tribunal asked the clerk to explain the elements contained in the offence for which Rebecca had been convicted.

'Is there any dishonesty in the offence?' the chairman queried.

'No,' replied the clerk. 'No dishonesty or intention is necessary.'

As they left the room to consider, Rebecca turned and smiled at Anne and Peter behind her.

'You did well,' Peter assured her.

'Did I miss anything?' she worried.

'No, you said it all,' Anne answered.

'Please stand,' said the clerk.

The tribunal was coming back in. Rebecca couldn't believe it. They had been out for about fifteen minutes. This can't be good news, she stressed. Rebecca looked down and prepared herself for their ruling.

The tribunal noted that the offence did not require dishonesty and that the case had not been put on those grounds. They took into account mitigation and the trial judge's sentencing remarks. Rebecca was not considered a risk to the public and the tribunal concluded that it would be disproportionate to strike her off the roll.

In the circumstances, we must mark the conviction with a sanction. We have decided that the appropriate punishment is suspension for 12 months and payment of the costs of £2000.

12 months? 12 months? Had she misheard? Surely they said 12 years? Rebecca started to cry, she was in shock, she turned and looked at Anne. She was in tears too. They both nodded at each other in disbelief. The tribunal retired and Rebecca jumped up to hug her parents. The tears today were of happiness. Rebecca had never cried with happiness before. She had become much more emotional since this whole thing started.

When she finally absorbed it, Rebecca turned to the clerk.

'I'm sorry, I was so shocked I didn't say thank you to them. Please tell them. And thank you, and you,' she said turning to the prosecutor.

Finally, people who can finally see it for what it was. Someone who wants to give me a chance, she thought.

As they left the Law Society, they were all on a high. Anne called Rebecca's aunties, uncles and grandparents. They were all over the moon. Rebecca wanted to call Steve straight away.

'I knew it!' he told her.

Everyone was genuinely so ecstatic about her news.

'That's fantastic,' Marie exclaimed.

'I've got my life back,' Rebecca replied. 'I can start again.'

Rebecca rang Duncan. His reference had been instrumental in the tribunal's decision. He was such a well respected and experienced member of the profession that his opinion would be taken seriously and have a huge amount of weight. He could have washed his hands of her as soon as she was arrested but he stood by her from the start and continued to support her after the conviction. She could not have had a better employer. She knew how lucky she was.

Never an emotional man, 'That's great news,' Duncan responded to Rebecca's news. She knew he was pleased but he was still upset by the jury's verdict. He felt that he had let Rebecca down in some way. Rebecca didn't feel like that at all. She knew he had fought for her. He had done his best and she would be eternally grateful.

Rebecca had to wait for the suspension to pass. Peter paid the costs for Rebecca and she set up a direct debit to repay him in instalments. She couldn't expect her parents to bail her out, they'd been doing it all her life and it had to stop. It was her fine and she had to pay it.

CHAPTER THIRTY

So much time had passed since the trial, that although Rebecca had just got her tribunal decision her suspended sentence was about to come to an end. She decided to celebrate with Steve. Their relationship had grown so close in such a short time. They had been friends for so long they didn't have to get to know each other first. They had a really strong foundation from the off. Rebecca knew that if it was to progress any further they would have to live near to each other. Travelling most weekends wasn't practical. It was expensive and tiring.

'I want to move back down there,' Rebecca told Anne.

Anne was worried.

'I don't feel like you're safe down there. I don't trust the police, I don't want you near *his* family. I think you are better up here.'

Anne didn't want Rebecca to move away. She was concerned about Rebecca's welfare. She felt that the police would always have a vendetta against her especially now that she had made a complaint against them. It was the first time in years that they argued. Rebecca knew that Anne was just trying to protect her. She hated that her mother was upset by her decision. Rebecca just wanted her life back. She needed to be around her friends and wanted to be with Steve. She couldn't do that while she was living with her parents.

Rebecca made the decision to move. Her parents were not happy but she was an adult and her mind was made up. It was arranged that she would stay a few miles out of the town. She could continue her job working from home.

Rebecca spent Christmas with Steve and her family. Her suspended sentence had lapsed and everything was really positive. Rebecca had regular contact with her work colleagues from the solicitors.

A couple of months after Christmas, Rebecca was called by Duncan.

'When is your suspension up?' he queried.

'September,' Rebecca replied.

'We would like you to consider coming back to work here when you are able to. Just think about it.' Rebecca got off the phone. She was so pleased that they valued her enough to want her back.

She wasn't sure that she wanted to be full time there. Being a solicitor made her a vulnerable target and she never wanted to be in a position like that again. She was paranoid about the police and was over cautious about everything. She knew she would always be watched. Did she want to walk back into the court and police station? Rebecca wasn't sure but it was definitely something she would consider.

Peter sent Rebecca's post down to her. Some letters had still not been redirected properly. Rebecca recognised the handwriting. It was Raj. It was a belated Christmas card. He had written inside it, telling her that he would always love her. She still cared about him but she loved Steve now. It had been six months together and she could see this being it. Rebecca decided just to ignore the card. She hadn't heard from Raj for nearly a year. He didn't know about her and Steve and she would rather avoid the conversation if possible.

The following week, Rebecca saw a familiar number on her mobile. It was Raj. She answered. They chatted and asked how each other were. Rebecca was on edge. She knew she couldn't lie to Raj. She didn't want to. Now he had called she had to tell him that she was with Steve.

'Look,' she told him, 'I'm seeing someone. It's Steve.'

Raj laughed. 'Are you joking? He's not good enough for you. You can't be with him.'

'Well I am,' she responded. 'We get on well and I really like him.'

'He's just a joke,' Raj seethed. 'I thought you were better than that.'

Raj's tone became angry. 'You can't be with him.'

'I'll be with who I want. You can't tell me what to do.'

The call ended abruptly on bad terms. She knew she would have to have that conversation one day, she had just hoped it would be later rather than sooner. She didn't want to hurt Raj but she had to move on with her life and he couldn't tell her who she could be with. Rebecca knew the problem. It was because Raj knew Steve. She was always known as HIS girl, Raj felt that Steve was disrespecting him by being with Rebecca. She had kidded herself that Raj might care that she was happy and put her feeling before his. He loved himself too much to do that. He was his number one.

Rebecca called Steve that night. She could hear by his voice that something was wrong.

'Raj called me,' he told her. 'He told me I had to finish things with you.'

Who does he think he is? Rebecca thought. He's in prison and he thinks he can call the shots.

Rebecca was fuming. Steve had been intimidated by Raj. He told him he would finish it with Rebecca but he couldn't do it. He already loved her.

The calls continued from Raj. The warning and demands turned into threats. Raj tried to scare Steve into leaving Rebecca. He didn't call Rebecca again. For the first time, Rebecca was angry with Raj. She was starting to hate him. It was like a sudden realisation about the sort of man he really was. He didn't care about anyone apart from himself. 'How dare he think he has any say on my life any more,' she seethed.

'Why can't he let me go and be happy?' she asked Steve. She realised that is wasn't really about her. It was about Raj feeling a fool. It was his stupid male pride. That was always his downfall and things hadn't changed. He hadn't learned from his time in prison. He was exactly the same.

Rebecca wrote a letter to Raj asking him to put her first and accept her and Steve. She got an abusive, threatening letter back calling her a slut and a slag for moving on with someone else. Rebecca understood that their feelings had been rekindled during the trial but they had decided that it could never work and finished things months ago. She hadn't cheated. They weren't together. She had been honest. She wished now that she'd just kept him in the dark about it.

Steve received threats on his phone... is this address familiar? it asked. It was the address of Steve's family. Steve felt worried. He would deal with what Raj did to him but needed to protect his family.

Rebecca persuaded Steve to change his number. He was living at a different address now so there was no way Raj could reach him.

Time passed and Steve still thought regularly about the threats and promises of violence when Raj was released from prison. It was hanging over him. He knew the day would come when he would have to face Raj.

'It's years until his release, we will deal with it then,' Rebecca reassured him. 'He is not controlling my life any more.'

Rebecca went into town one Saturday with Marie and Jennifer for a spot of shopping. As Rebecca waited outside the changing rooms for her sister and friend, she spotted a familiar face walking towards her. It was Suri. Rebecca hadn't seen her since the trial. Suri walked past Rebecca and then turned back, 'I thought that was you,' she scolded. 'Thanks for doing that to Raj,' she added as she was scurrying away.

Rebecca could not believe the cheek! 'Thanks to him for dragging me into all that shit!' she yelled back across the shop. Suri must be absolutely deluded! How dare she criticize Rebecca for cutting contact with Raj and meeting someone else.

'It was your own fault you got involved with him,' Suri replied as she walked towards the exit. She would not stop and confront Rebecca. Rebecca suspected it was her loyalty to her brother that had made her say anything at all.

'Oh yes,' Rebecca bellowed, 'poor Raj, he's done nothing wrong!' He was being treated like the victim in this. Rebecca was seething. She felt angry that Suri did not have the guts to stop and have it out if there was a problem. She had just made her comment and practically run out of the shop.

Rebecca looked around her and saw that people in the shop had stopped what they were doing and were staring at her. 'I'm really sorry.' She smiled. She was so embarrassed. She did not want to be in the middle of a scene, yelling across a busy shop.

'What the hell just happened?' Marie rushed out of the changing rooms still putting her arm through the sleeve of her top. She had heard it all. 'It was Suri,' Rebecca told her. 'I cannot believe the audacity of that family.' Marie was outraged.

CHAPTER THIRTY-ONE

Before Rebecca and Steve had got together, Steve had applied for the Navy. He wanted a career with opportunities and wanted to travel. He had undergone physical endurance tests, mentally challenging exam questions and medicals. He had put a lot of hard work into getting accepted and was focused on where he wanted to be.

Steve was waiting for his start date to begin his training in Portsmouth. Rebecca was sad that he was going to be away a lot but had high hopes that they were strong enough to last.

Steve finally got his start date a year into their relationship. They both knew it was coming but had put it to the back of their minds. They had decided that they would go on a goodbye holiday when they knew the date. It was now time. They booked a last minute trip away to return just a few days before Steve was due to leave.

They had an amazing time together and it cemented in Rebecca's head that Steve was the one for her. Towards the end of the holiday Steve made a confession to Rebecca. 'I don't want to go.' Rebecca had wanted to hear those words since they had been together but would never have asked him to stay. He had to do what he wanted and she didn't want him to regret it later in life.

'Are you absolutely sure?' Rebecca pried.

'I've just been waiting for you to tell me not to go,' he replied. Rebecca laughed. They had both been feeling exactly the same but hadn't wanted to be the one to say.

Steve contacted the training centre and told them he would not be coming. He felt a huge sense of relief. He had a new life and focus now with Rebecca. What he was looking for with the Navy he no longer had the need for. Steve's decision told Rebecca everything she needed to know. They were both committed to each other and could look to a future together.

Three years on and Rebecca and Steve are now married. They have not heard from Raj directly but have heard through various sources of his plans for them both on his release. 'He's after your blood,' Rebecca was told on a night out. Rebecca told herself there was no point in worrying until or if something happened. 'What a sad man,' she told herself. She couldn't quite believe that she'd thought that there was a decent person in there for all those years. She saw him now for the monster he was.

Rebecca has been working back at Harters for the past couple of years. It was like she had never been away. At first, she found it hard working back with the police who had put her through hell. They were all the same to her. She found it hard to see the good in any of them. She did not trust a single officer and treated them all with the same contempt. She also had to face those who had gossiped and talked about her behind her back. She learnt to be civil and professional but to keep the relationship purely on that level. She did not need to be friendly with anyone that had doubted her. Rebecca really can sympathise with clients while they are going through proceedings. She truly knows how they feel when they can't sleep or eat before their day in court.

Funnily enough, Rebecca saw many people who tried to pretend that they were worried about her and were glad to see her back. She knew that they were exactly the people who had been spreading the rumours and bathing in her misery. 'Keep your enemies close,' Rebecca told herself through gritted teeth.

To this day, Rebecca feels anxious when the postman knocks on the door early in the morning or if there is a police car behind her in the traffic. It's like a post-traumatic stress from everything that she has been through. It's probably something that will never entirely go away. She has moments of irrational worry and has to talk herself down. The trouble is that she knows only too well that irrational thoughts can actually become reality. Anne raised the possibility of counselling with Rebecca but she flattened the idea. 'I'm fine, Mum, I don't need it.' Rebecca was going to deal with it herself and put the past behind her.

She's still reminded of her past from time to time. She has come a long way since then. It taught her a lot and made her a lot stronger. She's now looking forward to a happy and positive life with Steve.